Pr — The Dahlonega Sisters – The Gold Miner Ring

"*The Dahlonega Sisters* is such a fun and delightful read, I want to get to know the three sisters in real life."
—Jeanne Felfe, author of *Bridge to Us*

"The bond between the Dahlonega sisters is secured by celebrating their differences in the mist of conflict and heartache. The story symbolizes how answers to the past can pave the way for the future not only for these women, but for us all."
—Nicki Jacobsmeyer, Author of *Images of America: Chesterfield*, Arcadia Publishing

"This delightful novel twists and turns with comedy, romance, tugged heart strings, mystery and more. *The Dahlonega Sisters* entertains on every page."
—Tammy Lough, Award-Winning Author and Romance Columnist at DIYMFA.com

The Dahlonega Sisters

The Gold Miner Ring

Diane M. How

Silver Lining Publishing, L.L.C.

ST. PETERS, MISSOURI

Published by Silver Lining Publishing, L.L.C.
70 Oakridge West Drive
St. Peters, Missouri 63376 (United States of America)

Publisher's Note: This is a work of fiction. Names, characters, places, and incidents are a product of the author's imagination. Locales and public names are sometimes used for atmospheric purposes. Any resemblance to actual people, living or dead, or to businesses, companies, events, institutions, or locales is completely coincidental. Although some real-life iconic places are depicted in settings, all situations and people related to those places are fictional, as is the gold miner ring and the "History of the Gold Miner Ring."

Book Layout © 2017 BookDesignTemplates.com
Book Formatting by Jeanne Felfe
Cover Design by Jennifer Quinlan of Historical Editorial
Cover Photos: iStock and Adobestock

Publisher's Cataloging-in-Publication Data provided by Five Rainbows Cataloging Services

Names: How, Diane M, 1951- author.
Title: The Dahlonega sisters : the gold miner ring / Diane M How.
Description: Saint Peters, MO : Silver Lining Publishing, 2019. | Also available in ebook format.
Identifiers: LCCN 2019914439 | ISBN 978-1-7340383-0-9 (paperback) | ISBN 978-1-7340383-1-6 (ebook)
Subjects: LCSH: Sisters--Fiction. | Superstition--Fiction. | Older women--Fiction. | Women--Fiction. | Georgia--Fiction. | Small cities--Fiction. | Humorous stories. | BISAC: FICTION / Family Life / Siblings. | FICTION / Women. | FICTION / Humorous / General. | FICTION / Southern. | GSAFD: Humorous fiction. | Love stories.
Classification: LCC PS3608.O8965 D34 2019 (print) | LCC PS3608.O8965 (ebook) | DDC 813/.6--dc23.

This book is dedicated to a remarkable woman and my dear friend, Vincenne Caruso, fondly known as Mutzi. Although the story is not the one she shared with me, it planted the seeds from which this novel grew. Mutzi (pronounced moot see) also generously allowed one of the characters to adopt her delightful nickname.

Dahlonega, Georgia

Most everyone has heard of the forty-niners, people who rushed to California when gold was discovered. Few people realize the first official gold rush in the United States occurred twenty years earlier in Dahlonega (pronounced duh lon eh ga), Georgia.

The quaint, historical town in Northeast Georgia attracts visitors from across the nation during the Gold Rush Days Festival held in October. Right in the middle of the bustling town square is the Dahlonega Gold Museum. The many attractions and delightful residents made this town perfect for the McGilvray sisters.

Even though the women adopted some familiar names, all of the characters are fictitious. However, all of the venues mentioned existed when I wrote the book.

If you're looking for a new adventure where you can pan for gold, kayak down the Yahoola Creek, and nibble on scrumptious chocolate while sipping delicious wine, add Dahlonega, Georgia to your schedule.

Chapter One

Normal had never been used in the same breath as Mutzi McGilvray.

She removed the grocery items cradled in her oversized Christmas sweater and placed them onto the conveyor belt. The elfin-size woman brushed potato dust from her purple paisley leggings and smoothed down the hem of her curled-up pullover. Looking toward the ceiling, she counted, extending fingers on both hands until she ran out and starting over again with her left. "Ten, eleven, twelve. That should do it."

Her twin sister, who stood inches away and towered a foot taller, adjusted the expensive designer bag hanging on her shoulder, leaned down, and whispered in Mutzi's ear, "Normal people use a cart."

As a young girl, Mutzi's schoolmates goaded her with names like weird or crazy or worse. As she aged, more respectable words like colorful, non-conformist, idiosyncratic described her. Today, most referred to the over-sixty, silver-haired shopper as eccentric.

Mutzi narrowed her eyes and glared at the stalker. "Back off, Marge."

Grocery shopping at Fresh and Frugal normally

came under Marge's purview. Always had. She masterfully controlled the kitchen and all the meals. Mutzi didn't mind, in fact she appreciated it. Still, today's close scrutiny chafed her nerves like an irritating tag sewn into the neckline of a blouse. Marge needn't concern herself with Mutzi's plan for the objects. She'd find out soon enough.

It became clear Marge wasn't going to move, her eyes still focused on the hodge-podge of goods. Mutzi stepped back. She'd considered jabbing her sister with an elbow, but with her luck, she'd damage Marge's trendy new camel-colored suit, the one that matched her stylish beige blouse, taupe shoes, and surely her underwear. It wasn't worth it. Clothes were important to Marge. As President of Dahlonega's Woman's Club and a member of the Historical Society, she had an image to uphold within her Georgia hometown.

Mutzi prided herself on having a different style. She found her best pieces at thrift stores and yard sales, putting them together in absurdly interesting ways.

The more vibrant the color and pattern, the better. Truth be told, dressing for shock helped keep people at bay, and she needed her space. Besides, shaking things up added spice to her life. So what if people whispered when she walked by? Who were they to design the size or shape of her box?

It seemed odd to Mutzi that society found it normal for a woman to push a finicky cat in a stroller, as if it were a baby. And how often had she seen dogs dressed in costumes and pranced around in parades? But how dare she wear two different colored socks or stripes with polka dots. For goodness sake, that's downright ostentatious.

Marge's eyes widened and a gasp escaped her mouth as she lifted a small bottle. "Gin? You're drinking gin now?" She scanned past the apples and potatoes and grabbed the two bags of chocolates. "I hope you're not planning to eat these. What about your blood sugar? It'll skyrocket."

Mutzi rubbed the back of her neck. "Don't get your panties in a bunch. They're not for me. They're for a project I'm working on." She watched as the cashier placed a box of gold raisins and some yellow crackers shaped like fish into her reusable bag.

Marge set the alcohol down. "Have you been on the internet again? Remember the last time you tried to bake something?" Marge's hands flew to her cheeks. "You almost burned down my lovely Victorian."

"Put a sock in it, Margaret Ann." Mutzi grabbed her grocery bag and sprinted toward the exit. "You keep sewing your perfect little placemats. I'm doing something new and creative." She left and headed toward the Dahlonega Visitor Center.

The streets in the town square were filled with slow moving cars and people dodging in between them. The sweet smell of chocolate drifted from the The Fudge Factory, tickling her nose. A scarecrow, made to look like George Washington, greeted shoppers as they hurried inside to buy their favorite candies.

The scarecrows had become a fall tradition sponsored by the Dahlonega's Woman's Club, of which Mutzi was also a member. Local vendors paid to participate in the competition each year. Prizes were awarded for the best decorated display. The event brought hundreds of visitors from miles away and each year the theme changed. This year showcased United States presidents. Mutzi enjoyed being part of an event where the proceeds helped secure scholarships for many students attending the local college.

A large red firetruck in the Giggle Monkey Toys store caught Mutzi's attention long enough for Marge to catch up with her.

"Did you see the Lincoln scarecrow?" Marge pointed toward the Dahlonega Gold Museum.

"Sure did. It's the best as far as I'm concerned."

Mutzi stared at the likeness of the sixteenth president—her favorite because he was such an odd duck. "Wonder where they got Abe's stovepipe hat? Don't see those anymore."

"Not sure, but it looks authentic." Marge glanced around the town square and smiled. "Nearly every venue participated this year." She pointed to PJ's Rusted Buffalo leather store. "Even Clyde Jones designed one for his place."

Mutzi turned and walked toward it. "*Some* people have great imaginations." The dig brought no response from Marge. Not a surprise. Most often, she accepted Mutzi's pokes and silly quirks. Still, there were days when Mutzi knew she'd gone too far, like the unfortunate kitchen fire and the time she set off the smoke alarm in the middle of a cold, rainy night just to remind the family they needed to prepare an emergency exit plan.

Her brain didn't work quite like everyone else's. Besides her unique attire and unfortunate mishaps, superstitions played a large part in Mutzi's daily decision process, too. Tomatoes eaten on Tuesday would bring bad luck all day, often putting a kink in Marge's menu planning. Killing a bee that entered the house meant a week of disasters. If three people were photographed together, the one in the middle would die first. Mutzi would pose with one sister or the other, but never the three together.

Everyone dismissed her fears as silliness, but no one knew the skeleton in the cupboard that brought the most terror to her life. If things worked as planned, she'd be rid of it soon.

"Morning, Ladies." The almost bald, short-stack of a man swept the sidewalk as he spoke in a slow southern drawl. His deep-furrowed, pruned face hinted at his age.

The sisters responded in unison, "Morning, Clyde."

"Better get those plants in tonight. Gonna frost, ya know."

Mutzi shook her head. "Not for another eight weeks." Her ability to predict the weather was never in doubt. At least not in her own mind.

Marge chimed in, "I heard on the news there was a possibility—"

"I've been right for more than forty years. Think I know what I'm talking about, Sis." Mutzi shoved a hand in the air with her thumb pointed toward the Dahlonega General Store, leaving her sister to chat with Clyde. As she walked away, she called out, "I need to pick up something I ordered."

Once inside the store, she set her grocery bag by the check out. "I'll be right back, Geraldine. Need to get a few things."

She breezed down an aisle looking for shiny, metallic-gold, wrapping paper. "Better take a bunch," Mutzi muttered to herself, as she often did, whether at home or out in public. She headed to the back of the store where she found the proprietor straightening items on a shelf.

"Hey, Harvey. Got those bricks for me?" She chuckled at the genius idea she'd planned out weeks ago. The store owner had laughed, too, when she'd put in her request.

With a nod, he scurried off into a back room and returned. "You needed twelve, right?" The man with a Santa Claus beard handed Mutzi a large onion sack stuffed to the brim with empty boxes. "Think these will work?"

Mutzi peered into the bag and pulled one out. The wide variety of sturdy cardboard cartons was exactly what she needed. "Perfect." She gave him a nod and ambled toward the checkout lane.

"Got enough tape?" Geraldine inquired with a tilt of her head, one hand rubbing her distended belly.

"Ooh. Thanks for reminding me."

"It's right there, on the endcap."

"Add 'er up, girl. Gotta get home and get this going. Need ten days for the raisins to soak."

Geraldine laughed so hard her round, pregnant belly jiggled. "Might have to buy one of those gold bricks just to see what else you've got up your sleeve."

"This year I'm going to bring in the most money for the club. You wait and see." Mutzi slung the sack over her shoulder and picked up the grocery bag.

"Can you make it home with all that?"

"Shucks, this is a breeze compared to those fifty-pound sacks of potting soil I hauled last month."

Geraldine shook her head. "You're something else."

"That's what they tell me. Have a good day."

A cool wind whipped across Mutzi's face when she stepped outside. Marge was nowhere in sight. "Probably already home talking to the dead." It drove Mutzi crazy to hear her sister chatting away to a picture every day like the man was still alive. Guess it's hard to let go after forty-five years.

Mutzi hoped Marge had plans for the day. She wanted her out of her hair long enough to get this project underway without her offering some snide remarks. The two block hike up the precipitous incline winded Mutzi. She paused to rest, setting the grocery bag on the pavement for a second. It toppled over and sent apples scattering down the steep grade she'd just conquered.

"Crap!" Mutzi ran zigzagging down the hill trying to catch up to the wayward fruit. The sack full of boxes, still slung over her shoulder, ricocheted from her chest to her back with every stride. After capturing the last apple, she glanced up and realized she was nearly back to where she'd started. "Ugh. Double crap." She huffed and puffed as she pounded her way back up.

By the time she climbed the white porch steps leading to the front door of the house she shared with Marge, she plopped the bags down and collapsed onto the wooden swing. Closing her eyes, she tried to catch her breath. The screen door creaked open, but she continued rocking. It didn't take long before the steady rhythm of the porch swing lulled her to sleep.

Chapter Two

*M*arge studied the curious mixture of items as she took them out of Mutzi's bag and set them on the kitchen counter. What in the world did her sister have in mind? She'd let her nap for a while and then they'd have a talk. Marge couldn't have her sister embarrassing her at the Gold Rush Days Festival. The Woman's Club would kick Mutzi out and then what would she have to do with her life, besides sit behind that crazy computer feeding her outlandish superstitions?

It wasn't long before Mutzi came rushing into the kitchen. When she saw all her purchases spread across the island, she let out a "whew" and slapped a hand across her heart.

Marge rolled her eyes and continued to cut up vegetables, tossing them in a crock pot. "What's with the drama?"

Mutzi heaved a sigh and sat down on a stool. "I already chased the darn fruit halfway down the hill once. Sure didn't want to have to do it again." She picked up an apple and examined it. "Thanks for bringing in the stuff."

"I thought you could use a hand. Feeling better?"

Her sister wiped at her eyes and smoothed her hair. "Climbing that hill is hard enough some days, but doing it twice is a bi—bummer."

Marge sent Mutzi a stern scowl, but held her tongue. She didn't tolerate cursing. Picking up one of the apples, she inquired, "Are you planning on making a pie with these?"

"No. Not me, but..." Mutzi rearranged some of the items. "Look. I wanted to surprise you, but since you did something nice for me, I'll let you in on my plan." Mutzi picked up one of the boxes and the foil paper. "I'm turning these into gold bricks and each one of them is going to have a different surprise inside."

Marge set the apple down on the marble island and reviewed the items. "I see a theme. Yukon Gold's, Golden Delicious Apples, even chocolates wrapped like gold nuggets."

A grin spread across Mutzi's face. "That's right. Gold Rush Festival...get it?"

"I get the connection." Marge sighed. "You know, not everything has to be gold, Mutzi."

The smile faded from Mutzi's face. "Don't you worry about it. I know what I'm doing. This is going to be great."

Marge bit on the inside of her cheek, hesitant to say anything else. Yet, the strong need to help her sister realize the consequences pushed her to continue.

"You're going to put perishable food in the boxes? Is that a good idea? The festival's still two weeks away."

Mutzi slammed down the box. "There's your condescending attitude again. I knew better than to tell you. You always criticize everything I do, then wait for me to fail."

Marge's temples pounded with the accusation. "I do not!" She whipped off her apron and crumpled it up, tossing it on the island as she glared at her sister. "I simply encourage you to think things through." Picking up the apron again, Marge smoothed it out and hung it on a hook, releasing a quiet sigh. "Sometimes you do silly things."

"Well, I'll do whatever the heck I want." Mutzi tried to work out the crease she'd put in the box and put it back in the onion sack. "This is going to be the talk of the festival. You'll see."

"Let's just make sure the talk is favorable." Marge moved toward the foyer and picked up her purse. "I've got a meeting at the Historical Society. I'll be late." She swung a buttercup-colored shawl over her shoulders before heading out the door. "Dinner's in the crock."

"Dinner's in the crock," Mutzi sassed in a sing-song voice, wobbling her head from one ear to the other, doing a prissy little dance. "Yeah, yeah, yeah. Oh course it is, Ms. Perfect, with every auburn-dyed hair in place and your impeccably coordinated clothes and jewelry, even matching lipstick." She pretended to primp, mocking her twin. "Sometimes you make me sick."

So what if Mutzi's last project had been a complete failure. She'd spent hours on the computer making all those beautiful signs to post around town, telling folks about the Fourth of July celebration. They looked great until the rain came. Been a drought for months. It wasn't her fault it chose to rain the week before the event. The words on every one of those darn signs ran like syrup on a pancake. "Not this time. I'll show her."

Mutzi located a plastic disposable container in the pantry. She emptied the golden raisins into it and opened the small bottle of gin, pouring it over the wrinkled fruit. "Just enough time for them to ferment before the festival." With the lid sealed, she wrapped a few layers of tissue paper around the outside, just in case the liquid leaked, and placed it in one of the boxes.

The bags of chocolate nuggets didn't quite fill any of the boxes, so she nestled them in tissue paper, too and stuffed them in the smallest box. She measured the shiny gold wrapping paper and cut it with precision. After taping it in place, she stood back and studied the finished products. "Not too bad. Two down. Ten to go."

She picked up the Gold Bond hand cream next and repeated the process, stacking the third brick on top of the others. Before she started on the fourth box, she reached for the worn binder that held her mother's favorite recipes. She flipped the pages until she found the two recipes she wanted, one for apple crumb pie and one for her mom's treasured potato casserole. She copied them onto decorative three-by-five cards.

"Every person in town would pay big bucks to get these bricks if they knew they held Mom's secret recipes." What was Marge worried about? People store potatoes and apples in dark places for months. These should be fine. She continued to reassure herself, humming a little tune as she worked.

The apples required a larger box. "People think the bigger, the better. This one will sell first, so it needs to be extra special." Mutzi searched the pantry with a keen eye. She selected one of the five pie plates Marge kept on hand and inspected it for chips or cracks. "Looks like new to me. Marge will never miss it." She stuffed extra packing in the bottom of the box and when she was pleased with the contents, she sealed the huge gold brick, oblivious to the bruises forming on the fruit that had traveled the extra block downhill.

The sun had set by the time she finished the eleventh brick. The shiny boxes nearly filled the kitchen island. "Maybe I can get this last one done before Marge gets back." She went to her bedroom to find the final object. "Hope you don't mind, Dad. But this has to be done." Mutzi shook her head. "Oh, good Lord. I'm getting just like Marge, talking to the dead." She dug behind her unmentionables and pulled out a tiny velvet case, clutching it to her chest and looking over her shoulder to be sure she was alone.

The anxiety of holding it in her hand made perspiration form on her forehead. Ever since she took the ring, her life had fallen apart. The thing was cursed and she knew it. Guilt and remorse had kept her from getting rid of it, but it was time. She couldn't leave it behind and risk bringing pain to her sisters once she was gone. Maybe it would bring joy and good fortune to someone else.

The sound of the door slamming startled Mutzi and she stashed the case back into the drawer, smashing her finger when she slammed it shut. "Damn it!"

"I'm back, Sis."

Mutzi held her breath, hoping her sister hadn't heard her cursing. It was the one thing she didn't tolerate in her house. Anyone who broke that rule had to pack their bags and find another place to shelter.

"Be there in a minute." She pulled the door closed

as she left the room and then paused. It might be too obvious that she was trying to hide something. She opened it back up before heading to the kitchen.

Marge slipped the apron over her head and nodded toward the stack of gold bricks. "Looks like you've been very busy."

"Didn't even stop to eat." Mutzi began moving the boxes off the island, placing them in a corner of the study. "When I get done, I'll set the table."

Marge lifted one of the bricks and shook it gently, reminding Mutzi of when they were children and they'd find a wrapped present hidden in a closet. "I'm sorry about our disagreement earlier."

"Just sister fussin. It's okay." She took the box from Marge. "One more to go."

"You go ahead and finish. I can set the table."

There was no way Mutzi was going to wrap the last brick while Marge watched. She'd want to know all about it and that was never going to happen. *Once it's out of this house, the damage will be finished, although, the harm it's already caused can never be undone.*

Chapter Three

A prideful smile inched across Mutzi's face as she passed dozens of violet and blue blotch pansies embedded along the sidewalk in front of the Dahlonega Community House. She paused, remembering the many hours she and the rest of the Woman's Club had spent planting in preparation of the Gold Rush Festival. Vibrant yellow and deep rust-colored mums, offering the slightest hint of a soft, musky fragrance, spilled from large half barrels. "Good job, ladies."

"Fine job, for sure."

The unexpected voice startled Mutzi.

Reverend Mitch, pastor of St. Luke's Church, raised an eyebrow and grimaced. "Sorry. Didn't mean to scare you. Such a beautiful day I thought I'd take a walk."

"Yeah, it'll be nice weather for the next few days."

"Hope so." He squinted his eyes and studied the flowers along the building. "Are those daisy mums?"

"The ones with the white petals and yellow centers are." Mutzi pointed to the nearest barrel. "These are called Footballs." Mutzi thought for a moment. "Bet you didn't know there's more than 10,000 varieties of chrysanthemums?"

The reverend chuckled. "No. I didn't know that."

Fueled by his response, Mutzi continued, "Then you probably didn't know that in China, on the ninth day of the ninth month, which by the way is named Chrysanthemum, they have a holiday to celebrate these very flowers." Mutzi thrust her shoulders back and raised her chin. "How about that?"

"You're a walking book of knowledge, Mutzi. You always teach me something new."

"Read it on the internet." Finished with her lesson, Mutzi turned toward Marge's open trunk to retrieve the last of the gold bricks. Toying with her captive audience, she exaggerated a groan and pretended to struggle lifting one of the boxes.

The reverend rushed to her aid. "Let me help you."

Mutzi released a belly-laugh. "I'm just teasing. They aren't heavy, they just look that way." She gathered the remaining boxes in her arms. "You could close the trunk for me."

The reverend shook his head and chuckled. With a tip of his hat, he added, "You are one of a kind, Ms. McGilvray. Good day."

"Yes, I am." Mutzi continued to giggle as she made her way into the building. She paused, glancing around, pleased with the improvements made to the center since their last meeting. The scrumptious

aroma of sweet kettle corn diluted the hint of new car-
pet and paint scent that still lingered throughout the
spacious hall.

Their assigned tables were halfway between the
front door and the restroom, much to Mutzi's relief.
She plopped the boxes down on the end where Marge
busied herself arranging the display of placemats and
napkins, probably for the fiftieth time.

"Is that everything?"

"Yep. All twelve of them."

With that, Marge grabbed her purse. "I need to
run. See you later."

The morning shift had seemed like the right choice
for Mutzi when she volunteered for it. Her sister
would return to relieve her when the crowds grew
heavy by midafternoon. Crafts, gift baskets and ornaments, donated from the other club members, already
covered their assigned display area. Mutzi decided to
stack some of Marge's neatly-spread treasures, to
make room for her gold bricks. She found enough
room for ten of the boxes, so she tucked the other two
under the table, until later.

As people wandered by, Mutzi teased them with
the mystery of what each one contained. "Whatcha
think, Mabel? Take a chance on one of these lovely
gold bricks? No losers. They all contain something really special."

"Well, there is a little gambler inside of me. Maybe I'll take...this one!" She grabbed one of the flatter boxes.

Mutzi had no idea what she'd put in the box. "I hope you enjoy it. Let me know later what you got."

"Oh, I'm opening it right now. I can't wait until I get home. The curiosity would kill me!" She tore the gold wrapping off in one swoop and used a brittle nail to rip through the taped box flap.

Mutzi chuckled at her enthusiasm. "You got the golden raisins soaked in gin. The recipe's on the bottom of the container."

"Well, for Heaven's sake. Why'd you ruin a perfectly good box of raisins?"

"Wait till you try them! I read on the internet that if you eat eight of them every day, your arthritis will vanish."

"You don't say? Well, I don't usually imbibe, except for a thimble of wine now and then, but it might be worth a try. These cool days are killing me. I'll let you know if it works. Might have a new fundraising idea if it does." The woman laughed heartily and then shoved the box toward Mutzi. "Hold this. I have to pee. I'll be right back."

Mutzi grinned as she watched Mabel waddle to the restroom.

Max, the house janitor, eyed Mutzi and nodded toward the raisins. "Are there any more of those?"

"No. But there are lots of other good things. Want to buy one?"

The man rubbed his bushy beard and checked out the selection. "I'll take the big one."

"Good choice. The missus will love it, and so will you. Why don't you wait until you get home and share the surprise together?"

"I think I'll do that. Thanks."

Under her breath, Mutzi exclaimed, "I made two sales, the first two sales." Word spread fast and by noon all the gold bricks on the table were sold. She hated to admit it, but the competitiveness that used to drive the two sisters apart as children still surfaced now and then. She couldn't wait until Marge arrived and learned of her success.

"Can you tell me how much these are? They're the same color as my kitchen" The blue-haired woman held up one of Marge's sunflower yellow placemats.

"The price is listed on..." Mutzi realized another shopper blocked the sign she'd posted. She dug under the table for a notebook she'd tossed aside. Unable to find it, she felt her face flush. "Um. How about $20 for four of them. Does that sound reasonable?"

"I'll take them. And these napkins that match. How much are they?"

Flustered, she dug under that table again in vain. She thought for a moment, reasoning that Marge must have taken the notebook with her. "Going to be a tough morning," she muttered.

The woman frowned. "What was that?"

"Twenty for the napkins, too. It took Marge a long time to make them look like Christmas trees."

The woman dug through her purse and shoved two bills toward Mutzi. "Got a bag?"

Mutzi rolled her eyes and brushed an errant strand of hair from her face. "Let me look."

"Oh, just forget it." The woman hurried off to the next table.

Three young girls wiggled and giggled at the end of the booth, picking up reindeer ornaments and engaging them in a pretend fight.

With her arms crossed, Mutzi mustered a stern look. "You break 'em, you buy 'em."

The girls dropped the items and scattered.

The crowd of shoppers multiplied and kept Mutzi harried the rest of her shift. She loved seeing all the people gather in Dahlonega for the festival, but it wore her out. The building seemed to shrink as the day went on making her feel claustrophobic.

When Marge arrived to relieve her, Mutzi fled with barely a goodbye, pushing her way through the congested hall into the busy streets outside. Worming her way around the mass of elbow-to-elbow shoppers frazzled her more. Sheer determination gave her the energy to make it to the street leading up to the massive hill.

The hike home left Mutzi's throat parched and the minute she reached the kitchen, she went straight to the fridge to find a cold drink. She eyed a brown bottle hidden behind the milk and made her selection. "Wonder how long this has been in there?" She studied the beer and found the born on date—2010. "Hmmf. Been here since George passed on." It was the one vice he'd indulged in during his bout with cancer. The painful memory settled in her mind. She walked to the study where Marge kept his picture and held the bottle up in salute. "This one's for you, George."

The Community Center buzzed with shoppers, their chattering drowning out the Christmas music playing in the background. Marge peeked in the metal cash box, pleased with the stack of bills that bulged out of it. She closed the lid and tucked it out of sight.

"Marge! Marge!"

The voice came from across the hall and it took Marge a few seconds to identify who was calling her name. A petite woman with overly applied cheek blush squirmed around shoppers until she reached the table.

"Hello, Mrs. Gibson. How are you today?"

"I am blessed. Always, blessed." Her slender face brimmed with a grin.

Marge nodded her head. She wouldn't have expected anything different from Annabelle. "Can I interest you—"

Annabelle interrupted and winked. "I just had to come back to tell Mutzi how wonderful the surprise was in my gold brick." She clasped her hands together and shrugged her tiny shoulders. "I'm going to save the paper, it was so pretty."

It was the first time Marge had heard anything about the bricks. "I'm sorry she's not here. She went home." She was almost afraid to ask about its contents, but curiosity compelled her to inquire. "What was in the box?"

"Oh, it was so lovely. It will fit my little table perfectly. I can't wait to show it off."

Marge smiled at the enthusiastic woman and asked again, "What did you find inside the brick?"

"Why, the most beautiful lace doily runner I've ever seen."

The words made Marge's mouth drop open. Mother's runner. Would Mutzi give away the runner Mother embroidered for her? "Was it gold?"

"Oh, yes, honey. Just perfect for Christmas. Please tell Mutzi thank you."

"I will. And thank you for supporting the Dahlonega Woman's Club."

No sooner had Annabelle left the table, another woman appeared carrying a large burlap bag, stuffed with various purchases.

"I can't believe I got such a treasure."

Marge had no idea what the woman referred to. "Treasure?"

The woman leaned in and whispered, "The secret recipe for your mother's delicious potato casserole."

Marge's hand flew to her chest. "Mother's recipe was in a gold brick?"

"Yukon Golds. After all these years, I wondered why I couldn't make that casserole taste just like your mother's. Now I know the secret. I'm going to make it for Sunday's dinner."

When the lady left, Marge searched all the tables, but could not find any of the gold boxes. *She really did sell them all. Good for her.*

The inside crowd dwindled as the evening festivities began outside. A bluegrass band started playing, signaling her shift was over and the center would be locked up until noon on Sunday.

With her purse in hand, Marge ventured out into the crowd of people gathered in the town square.

Many sat on blankets or folding chairs they'd brought from home. The band's rendition of White Christmas drifted up to the starlit sky. She considered finding a bench and listening for a while, but decided she hadn't dressed warm enough for the cool breeze that sent chills down her back. Instead, she headed home, excited to share the pleasant comments about Mutzi's bricks.

Only the foyer light was on when Marge walked in, a sign Mutzi had already turned in for the night. With Marge attending church in the morning and then working another shift at the festival, she wouldn't see her sister until the following evening. *I better fix something for her to eat in the morning or she'll just have toast for breakfast.* Mustering up the energy, she went to the kitchen and got started.

Humming White Christmas as she worked, Marge prepared a breakfast quiche to pop in the oven before leaving for church. Although her bones were tired, cooking always soothed her spirits. Attending Sunday Mass alone saddened her. She wished Mutzi would go with her, but she'd given up trying to convince her to return to her faith. *Maybe, some day.* She reached for a pen and jotted a note to her sister. *Have a great day. Food's in the oven.*

Marge waited on her last customer. Three more people had come by to reveal their pleasure with the purchase of Mutzi's bricks. One received a signed copy of Anne Dismukes Amerson's *Dahlonega, Georgia: Site of America's First Major Gold Rush*. Another received the unworn gold silk scarf Marge gave Mutzi one year for her birthday. No one had mentioned the apples. Checking under the table for empty cartons in which to store the few unsold items, Marge found two more gold bricks.

"Oh no, what if one of these has something perishable in it?" One of them was too light to contain apples, but the other weighed enough that it might. She dug into her purse and pulled out a large bill, adding it to the overstuffed money pouch. Glancing around, not wanting anyone to notice, she braved opening the heavier package.

Tucked in tissue paper were two gold candelabras, the ones from Mutzi's hope chest. "Oh, Mutzi." She remembered the day her sister bought them and how she'd planned to serve her future husband a candlelight dinner once a month. The thought that she would part with such sentimental objects broke Marge's heart. *Why would you give these away, Mutzi?*

With an urgency, Marge ripped open the second. Inside was a blue velvet box. She opened the lid and removed an unusual ring, slipping it onto her finger.

One of the newer club members walked up as Marge was studying the intricate design of a man panning for gold, sitting on white opal.

"That's pretty. I've never seen anything like it."

"I haven't either." She shook her head wondering if her sister had purchased it recently. "It's...so appropriate for this area." Marge looked up at the woman who had a puzzled look. "The first US Gold Rush happened here, in Dahlonega."

"I didn't know that. That *is* special."

"Yes. It is." Marge added under her breath, "So is my sister."

All the way home, Marge thought about the items Mutzi gave away, wondering if there was a deeper meaning to them. The lace doily runner and the candle holders had never been used, but surely held a sentimental place in her heart. Mother's recipes were special, but she'd never thought of them as valuable. Her sister had.

It pained Marge that Mutzi gave away such treasured items. It made her sad to think her sister had given up on ever falling in love and getting married, even though Marge knew the chances were slim.

As she climbed the steps to her house, she reached for the hand rail and the porch light lit up the shiny ring. She paused to admire it again, puzzled she'd never seen it before. Just as she opened the door, the strap on her designer purse broke, spilling its contents all over the porch. "For Heaven's sakes."

Apparently Mutzi must have heard her because she pushed open the front door and rushed to catch a tube of lipstick before it rolled down the stairs.

"I told you paying all that money for a purse was a waste."

"I can't believe it came apart." Marge stuffed the loose change and other items into the expensive, but now useless purse. "Well, it's going back first thing in the morning."

"What's in the box?"

Unsure how Mutzi would react to the response, Marge pressed her lips tight and paused. "Now don't get mad, but when I was packing up the leftover items, I found two gold bricks under the table that didn't get sold. I'm sure they would have, if I'd found them sooner. The others were a big hit."

"Fiddlesticks. I didn't have room on the table, so I stuck them under there. It got so busy I forgot to dig them out."

"Well, I bought them. Good job, Sis. I think your idea was well received."

Mutzi's eyes widened and she grabbed the box from Marge to look inside. "Oh, the candle holders." She pushed the tissue papers to the side, still searching for something.

"I'm surprised you decided to donate these."

"No reason to keep them and I can't take them with me."

The comment disturbed Marge. "Are you planning on going somewhere?"

Mutzi shrugged her shoulders.

"Well, I'm glad you've got them back." Marge could say nothing else. It wounded her that her sister never married. She'd lost interest in all men after her first love left for the war. She never mentioned him, but Marge sensed she'd never gotten over him. "Let's go inside and I'll fix us some dinner."

Mutzi stood firm, blocking the door, refusing to move, a scowl accenting the crow's feet around her eyes. "What was in the second box?"

Marge studied her sister. Sometimes she wished she knew what went on inside her head. Other times, she was glad she didn't know. Marge stuck out her hand and wiggled her finger. "This ring. I love how unique it is."

The vein in her sister's neck bulged. "Damn it!"

"Mutzi! Your language!"

"I don't believe you did this. You—ruined everything."

Marge shook her head. "Ruined what? Where'd you get this?"

"None of your damn business."

"I'll have none of that talk in my house."

Mutzi stormed inside and went straight to her bedroom, slamming the door behind her.

Chapter Four

*D*awn nudged its way through a sliver of the wooden blinds in Mutzi's room, hinting night's gloom was on the move. She rose, still rattled from her failure to dispose of the ring, and untangled the twisted sheets, spreading them across the bed as quietly as the sun inching above the horizon. Hoping morning would bring a fresh perspective to her troubles, she headed to the bathroom.

She wanted to be rid of the ring and all of its painful memories. The joy she'd naively anticipated it would bring had long ago been obscured by missed opportunities, unrequited love, and even death. Hidden in a drawer for years, the ring's power lay dormant, yet the shadows of destruction continued to haunt Mutzi. She wouldn't expose her sister to the same bad mojo.

Mutzi ran a comb through her thinning silver hair and stared in the mirror. What would she do now? If her sister learned where the ring came from, she'd never forgive Mutzi for the unthinkable sin she'd committed so many years ago. Marge always insisted Mutzi's fears were silly superstitions and a result of too much time spent on the computer. But they weren't. The ring was the reason nothing ever worked out right.

As she left the house, Mutzi counted each of the twenty-five cracks in the sidewalk as she stepped over them. She'd made the five-block walk to Agnes Mayer's house many times. She'd be house-sitting at Agnes' place for the rest of the week and hoped—no prayed—in her absence, Marge would forget about the ring. Mutzi slipped the key into the lock. When she pushed the door open and stepped in, four cats encircled her ankles. "Guess you'll get my mind off things." She reached to stroke the calico who mewed and nuzzled against her hand. "How about some food?"

Four other women from the Historical Society arrived in the parking lot of the Dahlonega Community Center, promptly at nine in anticipation of their thirty mile drive to Gibbs Gardens. Marge, the designated chauffeur, greeted each of them as they climbed into her car. With the last one in, Marge put the key in the ignition and said, "I can't wait to see the holiday decorations. I hear they are spectacular this year."

A chorused response, "Me, too," made Marge smile, happy she'd suggested the trip.

The women chattered about the successful festival

as they headed out of town. The treasurer, Brenda, announced from directly behind Marge, "Mutzi brought in the most money with her gold bricks."

The news brought a nod from Marge. "She'll be happy to hear that. She put a lot of thought into each surprise."

One of the ladies giggled. "I heard some of the apples didn't fare too well, but Max's wife sure was happy to get the recipe and the nice pie plate."

The words settled in, stirring Marge's memory. *That's where the other pie plate went. That little stinker.* She shook her head and released a subtle chuckle. "I was worried about the apples. When I was closing up on Sunday, I found two more of the bricks stashed under the table and bought them."

"Ooh." Brenda shot forward and grabbed hold of Marge seat. "What'd you get?"

With her right hand elevated, Marge wiggled her fingers to show off the gold miner ring.

"Wow. How unusual."

The women scrambled to see the ring and two of their noggins bumped. "Ow."

"Where in the world did Mutzi get it?"

A loud pop startled Marge before she could respond. The car jolted to the right with such force, she gripped the steering wheel trying to maintain control. "Oh, shit!"

Marge slammed the brakes, screeching, "Stop! Stop!" as the car came to a halt on the soft shoulder, just shy of a deep ravine. Her purse slammed into the dashboard, spilling its contents onto the floorboard and sending a tube of lipstick under the gas pedal. "For heaven's sake."

Whipping her head around to check on the other riders in the car, Marge stifled another yelp. "Is everyone all right?"

The ladies glanced at one another. Brenda took a deep breath and nodded. "We're all okay."

Gertie shook her head. "Marge, I can't believe you cursed."

Closing her eyes for a moment, Marge released a sigh, relieved no one was hurt. "Don't you dare tell Mutzi."

The women giggled and responded together, "Not a word."

The taut seatbelt threatened to strangle Marge. She released it and adjusted her blouse. "I can't believe this. I just bought new tires last month." Marge checked her mirror for traffic and got out, walking around to the passenger side to inspect the deflated tire. She shook her head in disgust and returned to the other side of the car.

"I'll keep watch while you all get out. It's too dangerous to stay in the car."

The other women unbuckled their seat belts. One by one, they made their way onto the road, standing in front of the disabled vehicle.

"Now what?" Gertie, the oldest of the bunch, asked.

Marge reached into the car and retrieved her phone and wallet from the floorboard. "I'll call roadside assistance."

Brenda squinted, peering down the street. "Ooh. We're really close to that antique store I've wanted to check out."

Eight wide, hopeful eyes stared at Marge. She rolled her eyes at the four silly faces. These women lived to treasure hunt. "Go ahead. I'll wait here."

"I'll stay with you," Gertie said as the others turned to go.

"No." Marge sighed. "Go ahead with them. I'll be fine. I'll come get you when the tire's fixed."

"Are you sure?" Gertie inquired.

"Yes. Go."

The giddy women hurried down the shoulder of the road as quick as their fashionable pumps could manage.

A tow truck arrived within fifteen minutes. The driver's tight t-shirt hugged his chest, concealing, but not hiding young muscles that rippled beneath it. He brushed back his wavy brown hair revealing a large dimple. "Morning, ma'am." He extended his right hand and locked eyes with Marge, the corners of his lips turned up—not quite a smile—but enticing.

Her breath caught in her throat as she read the name on his shirt. George. She blinked and regained her composure. Realizing the man was waiting for her keys, Marge handed them over.

He popped the trunk and turned to her. "You're having a bad morning," he said with a soothing, southern drawl. "Your spare's flat, too." Slamming the trunk closed, he pulled a rag from the snug, hip pocket of his jeans, and wiped his hands. "I can tow it down the street to Pete's. He'll get you fixed in no time." The young man opened the passenger door of his truck. "Hop in. I'll give you a ride."

Frozen in place, Marge considered the offer. Taking a ride from a stranger? She thought of the hundreds of news reports and warnings she'd heard over the years. Still, what was she to do? *She* had called him, and the sign on the door of his truck looked legitimate. Besides, his name was George. Her eyes drifted toward the sky.

As if the driver read her mind, a smile spread across his handsome face and he gave a three finger salute. "It's all good. Scout's honor."

Reassured, Marge moved toward the open door, and then halted, her eyes focused on the raised running board, guessing it would require more

movement than her pencil skirt allowed. She shim-
mied the hem an inch above her knees and tried to
step up. Unable to negotiate the distance, she turned
sideways, hiked it a bit higher, exposing a little thigh,
and tried again. The seam in the back of her skirt split
just as the young man stepped closer. He placed a
strong hand on Marge's bottom, giving her a boost,
and sliding her into the seat. His touch sent a flush of
heat to her face.

"Nice undercarriage," he said with a wink and
walked to the back of the truck to prepare her car for
the tow.

Once he was out of sight, Marge chuckled. *Shame
on him.* Yet, it felt good to have a man notice her firm
bottom. Her husband had often said things like that
when he was alive. She'd missed hearing it. She giggled again. *Shame on me for letting him get by with that.*

When the muscled man finished hooking up the
tow and returned to the truck, Marge stared straight
ahead, hesitant to make eye contact for fear she'd
start giggling again. They rode in silence the few
blocks to the station.

George, Jr. turned toward Marge. "Here we are."

She cleared her dry throat and nodded. Grabbing
the door handle, she hesitated. If she moved it would
reveal the split in her skirt. How in the world was she
going to negotiate the distance to the ground? The

driver came around to the passenger side, opened the door and offered his hand. With as much dignity as Marge could muster, she accepted it and swung her legs to the right, planting both feet on the running board.

George kept his eyes focused on Marge's face as she lifted her skirt enough to step to the ground.

Exhaling the held breath, Marge straightened her jacket to cover the exposed area. "Thank you."

"*My* pleasure." The driver bowed and closed the door. His pearly white teeth gleamed as he pointed to the front entrance of the building.

Without waiting for him to unhook her car, Marge hurried into the service station restroom and dug into her purse for a few safety pins. After performing damage control on her skirt, she returned to the lobby. Pete, the service station manager, motioned to her to come into the garage where her car sat elevated on a rack with the wheel removed.

"You've got more problems, lady. Your brake line is leaking."

Both of Marge's hands clasped her cheeks. "You've got to be kidding."

"You're looking at two hundred bucks and a couple hours. I wouldn't suggest driving until it's fixed."

Shaking her head in dismay, Marge responded, "Well, I don't have a choice. Please get started as soon as you can. I've got a group of women waiting for me at the antique store down the street."

Pete rubbed his chin. "My nephew needs to get some parts from a store near there." The mechanic pointed to the corner of the office. "You can wait here, or he can give you a ride and come get you when it's done."

Another ride with a stranger? Marge glanced at the greasy, white—at least, she thought, it may have been white at one time—plastic lawn chair in the corner. "I'll take the ride. Thanks."

Marge stood near the antique store's window and checked her watch for the sixth time in fifteen minutes. It had been two hours since Pete's nephew had dropped her off. She felt foolish that she hadn't taken down the number of the business where her car had been towed. She had decided to ask the proprietor of the store for a phone book when the man returned. She hurried out to the car and they drove back to the service station, the radio blaring with hip-hop music.

Pete shoved a piece of paper toward Marge, a $400 bill for his services.

She frowned. "I thought you said $200?"

The burly man removed a stubby cigar from his

mouth with oil-black fingers. "It's all listed there, lady. Cash or charge. Don't take checks."

The bold letters on the bottom of the bill read *Friendly Highway Service*. "My foot," she mumbled. "It should say highway robbery." She fussed as she thrust her credit card toward him. Once the transaction was completed, Pete handed her the keys.

Marge steamed as she left the lot feeling like she'd been ripped off. By the time she picked up the other woman, it was too late to make the trip to the gardens. All Marge wanted to do was get home and go to bed.

Gertie leaned forward from the back seat and placed a hand on Marge's shoulder. "I'm starved. Let's stop in Dawsonville and have dinner."

Although Marge groaned, the growl in her stomach agreed, as did everyone else.

The house was dark by the time Marge pulled into her tree-lined driveway and parked. When she stepped out of the car, her foot settled on an errant pinecone and twisted, sending her plummeting to the ground, landing on her hip. "Ow!" She brushed gravel from her hands. "Great. Just what I needed."

She rolled over, balanced on her knees and used her hands to push up, managing to stand. The movement drew another yelp. "Ow!" Unable to put any weight on her left ankle, she hopped to the steps and pulled herself up, balancing on the ball of her foot. Finally inside, she dropped her purse on the hallway table and hobbled into the kitchen for an ice pack.

Marge picked up the phone to call Mutzi, and then put it back in its cradle. She knew her sister would come home to help her, but she didn't want to be a bother. Perhaps it would feel better by morning. She limped into the study and leaned her backside on the edge of the desk. "What a terrible day, George. I wish you were here. Things were so much easier when you were."

Stretching forward to pick up one of her favorite photos of her late husband, the one of him on the beach showing off his six pack, she felt her skirt pull tight.

A flashback of the tight-t-shirt-man made her smirk. *Well, maybe not everything is terrible.* Still, it made her miss her George more. "If you were here, you'd wrap your arms around me and hold me until I fell asleep." Marge set the picture back down. "It's getting late. I think I'm going to go to bed. See you tomorrow, love."

Mutzi was surprised to see Marge's car in the driveway when she stopped by the house the following day.

Normally, Marge would be gone to a meeting or out with some friends. She let herself into the house and found Marge's purse laying on the table in the foyer. She peeked in the kitchen. It was untouched from the previous morning, her dirty dishes still in the sink.

"Marge?" Mutzi hurried through each room and called again. "Hey, Sis?"

A muffled groan came from Marge's bedroom. Mutzi pushed open the door without knocking.

Marge hopped out of the bathroom on one foot and fell onto the unmade bed.

"What in the world happened?" Mutzi moved closer and poked a finger on Marge's swelled ankle.

"Ouch. Don't do that." Marge laid her head on the pillow and closed her eyes. With one hand across her forehead, she sighed, her eyes remained shut. "It's not that bad, really." Marge opened her eyes and tried to sit up, leaning against the headboard.

"Yesterday was a mess. I got a flat tire. Actually, two flats. The spare in the trunk was useless, too."

Mutzi grabbed another pillow and positioned it behind her sister's head. "Not a good start to your day trip."

"My skirt split getting in the tow truck. Then they found a leaky brake line." Marge's shoulders sagged lower with the accounting. "When I finally got home, I sprained my ankle getting out of the car."

"That sucks, I mean stinks." Mutzi picked up the limp icepack. "Do you want to go to the doctor?"

"No, no. I'm just exhausted from getting in the tub and dragging myself out. I'm sorry. I'm such a big baby."

"Stop that. You are not. You're tougher than anyone I know. I bet you haven't eaten either."

Marge closed her eyes again. "It'd take me another hour to work my way to the kitchen."

"Stay here. I'll refill the icepack and fix something." Mutzi moved toward the door. "You've got time for a nap. I'm not too fast, but I promise not to burn down the kitchen."

Marge opened her eyes and smiled. "Thanks, Sis."

Mutzi hurried to the sink and put on a fresh pot of coffee. Trying to decide what to fix, she settled on scrambled eggs, toast, and a fresh fruit salad. Nothing that required the oven. Fifteen minutes later, she put all of it on a bed tray, refilled the ice pack and headed to her sister's room.

Marge was sitting on the side of the bed when Mutzi entered. "That didn't take long. Look at you! What a fine breakfast you made."

"I'm glad to see you perked up." Mutzi watched as Marge took a fork full of eggs. Her stomach knotted the moment she noticed the ring on her sister's hand. "Did you wear that yesterday?"

"What?"

"The ring." Her voice strained to a higher octave. "Did you wear it yesterday?"

Marge held her hand up and wiggled her finger. "Yes. I was showing the ladies. They thought it was beautiful." She scrunched her face. "Come to think of it, I was showing it to them when the tire blew out."

Mutzi's chest tightened. "You need to take it off. Now."

Marge set the tray aside and turned to her sister. "What's wrong, Mutzi? What's with the ring?"

"It's cursed. Bad things happen. Trust me. I know. Look what happened to you since you wore it."

Marge flipped a dismissive hand at the suggestion. "Don't be silly. You know I don't believe in silly superstitions." She picked up her fork and stabbed at a strawberry. "If you want it back, just say so."

Mutzi looked up at the ceiling, tears threatening to breach. "I don't want the ring. I don't want it in this house. I told you, it's cursed." She stormed out of the room, shouting over her shoulder as she left, "It's not a superstition."

Chapter Five

Samuel Parks packed the final box of personal belongings. His and Song's house in Virginia had served them well since their military assignment to the states. It sold the first week on the market. After moving frequently with his Army career, Sam was eager to return to his hometown and plant himself in one place for his remaining years. As much as he grieved the loss of his wife, he was ready to move on.

Hundreds of friends had come from miles away to offer their condolences for Song Lee's passing. It was a testament to the number of people his wife touched during her life in the United States. She'd made an abundance of friends each time they were deployed to a new location.

Throughout their marriage, they'd discussed retiring further south, someplace warm. Sam's heart ached to suggest Dahlonega, Georgia, but he refused to propose it, even though Song would have loved the charm of the town square and the closeness of the people. She could have continued teaching English as a second language at the university, had she wanted to.

No, he'd caused enough heartache to his first love, the girl he'd abandoned when they were mere teens. He wouldn't risk showing up with another woman and causing more pain.

He loved Song for the strong, supportive woman she had been, but not a day went by that he didn't think of the one he'd left behind. At the very least, he owed her an explanation. Hopefully, she'd married and had children, lots of children, like she'd always dreamed of having. He prayed she'd had a happy, fulfilling life.

In the end, the plan to move back to Dahlonega had been Song's suggestion. She knew he still cared about the woman. When she received her terminal diagnosis, she talked to him about the woman who held his heart. She recognized the torch still burned strong in his heart and she encouraged him to return to let life unfold, however it was meant to be.

He'd started searching on-line for property to buy in the northeast Georgia mountain area. He'd lived his life following Colin Powell's words, "There are no secrets to success. It is the result of preparation, hard work, and learning from failure." While it served him well, he believed a greater force often made things occur. When he found out his family's ranch home, located outside the city of Dahlonega, was on the market again, it dissolved any lingering doubts.

In his dreams, Sam envisioned seeing Mutzi again, both of them older, but still in love with each other. He knew it was foolish to hold out hope, but something pulled him in that direction. In his weaker moments, he was sure she'd never forgive him for leaving. Sam closed the cover on the bed of his truck and took one last look around before driving off.

An unfounded excitement stirred inside him. A ridiculous fantasy, he told himself. Still, an old man could dream.

Chapter Six

*A*ttending an Ivy League college hadn't interested April Preston, although her mother, Rose Ellen McGilvray-Preston, insisted it would serve her better. April liked smaller towns and she'd always loved Dahlonega, where her two aunts lived.

With the help of a Hope Scholarship, April earned a Criminal Justice Degree from the University of North Georgia. With multiple opportunities for internships after graduation, she settled on a law firm in Dawsonville, a short commute from Dahlonega. Although her mother visited from New York only two or three times a year, April saw her aunts on a weekly basis. They always made her laugh and were known for giving sound, motherly advice.

April arrived at her aunts' home with two bottles of specially ordered wine from the Ole ' Mountain Collectables and Wine Store. Beaujolais nouveau, a palatable red, was only available once a year.

She'd been looking forward to Thanksgiving dinner at their house. It was her favorite meal of the year, a time when she'd enjoyed all the trimmings without worrying about what the calories would do to her slim figure.

Letting herself in without knocking, April made her way into the kitchen, breathing in the delectable aroma of celery and onion dressing baking in the oven. Pots bubbled on the six-burner stove and the once spacious kitchen island overflowed with casserole dishes and a steamy, golden brown turkey, juices oozing onto the platter.

Unaware she had company, Aunt Marge pinched the pie dough with precision, turning the dish and pinching it again and again, adding a delightful finishing touch to her masterpiece.

"I've already gained ten pounds just smelling all this food," April called out just as the oven timer buzzed.

Marge jumped, her head snapping toward April. "You could well afford it, Missy." She nodded toward a couple oven mitts on the counter. "The dressing's ready to come out of the oven. Want to get it for me?"

"You must have been up since dawn to make this big of a mess." April laughed as she teased her aunt, her brown pony tail swishing back and forth as she moved to the oven. She set the hot pan on the stove and crossed the room to wrap her aunt in a bear hug.

Marge raised her hands high. "Watch it. You'll be covered in flour. I'm a mess."

"It's worth a dusting to hug my favorite aunt."

Mutzi walked into the kitchen and chimed into the conversation. "I thought I was your favorite."

"Of course you are. You're twins. I love you both equally!" April kissed Mutzi's cheek as they embraced.

"Your aunt *has* been up since dawn. Looks like she's feeding an army."

April grabbed a spoon from the drawer and scooped a bit of the brown crust from the dressing pan. She dropped a bit on the floor and bent down to pick it up, catching a glimpse of Marge's wrapped ankle. "What happened?"

"Oh, just clumsy. Sprained my ankle coming up the front steps last week."

Mutzi crossed her arms and her face hardened. "Don't lie." The words flew from her mouth with venom. "You weren't being clumsy."

The tone shocked April. She'd never heard the two sisters quarrel. She blew little puffs on the spoon she held, waiting for the dressing to cool, and watched the interaction between them.

Marge ignored Mutzi's glare and turned on the hand mixer, attacking the mashed potatoes with an exaggerated determination.

April moved closer to Marge and settled her free hand on her aunt's shoulder. "Are you sure you're all right? I can take over from here."

"I'm fine. Don't worry." Marge nodded toward the

spoon. "Does the dressing need more salt?"

She nibbled on the sample. "OMG. This is your best ever."

Marge's cheek rose a bit. "You say that every year."

"Well, it's true. It's wonderful." April pulled out her phone. "I'm going to post a picture of your turkey. It should be on the front page of a gourmet magazine."

A full grin spread across Marge's face as she finished with the potatoes and picked up the last pie, popping it into the oven. "Great. Now every stranger in town will show up at the door for a free meal."

"Who are you kidding? You'd welcome them with open arms." Mutzi made her way to the stove. She reached into the pan and snatched some dressing.

"Well, it makes me happy to know people enjoy my cooking." Marge scowled at Mutzi. "You don't seem to mind it."

"No, I don't." Mutzi pursed her lips and huffed. "I need some air." She tossed the spoon into the sink and disappeared into the foyer.

April glanced from Mutzi as she left to Marge who lowered her head, avoiding eye contact. The visible tension made April uncomfortable. She moved to the sink, ran hot water and started washing pots and pans. The sun radiating through the window bounced off a shiny object sitting on the sill, drawing April's attention.

"That's a beautiful ring. I don't think I've ever seen it before. Is it new?"

Marge hobbled on her sprained ankle until she neared April. "It's new to me." She glanced toward the foyer and back. In a hushed voice, she whispered, "Remember the gold bricks Mutzi made for the festival?"

April nodded, wondering why the secrecy.

"I bought two of them and it was in one." Marge released a deep sigh. "I don't know where Mutzi got it, but she thinks it's—" Marge wrung the towel in her hand. "Something about it upsets her."

"Well, if you ever decide to get rid of it, send it my way." April laughed as she slipped the ring on her finger and admired it.

"Tell you what. It's yours. Just stick it in your pocket for now and don't mention it to Mutzi. I'd like us to get back to our old selves."

"Really? What's going on between you two?"

Marge shrugged her shoulders. "You noticed?"

"There's a definite edge to your conversations."

"Let's not talk about it anymore. I don't want to ruin a lovely day." Marge hobbled back to the stove and scooped the mashed potatoes into a serving dish.

Moving into the dining room, April noticed the cornucopia filled with orange and rust colored mums in the center of the table. "The flowers are beautiful. So festive for fall."

"They are lovely. Your mother sent them."

"She always picks out the best," April said, lightly touching one of the petals.

"We're going to need some extra space with all this food. Could you move them to the table in the foyer?"

"Sure."

Marge rearranged some of the bowls and plates on the table to make room for the turkey platter. When the last dish was placed, she called out, "Hey, Sis. It's time to eat."

Mutzi made her way into the dining room and looked around. "Where's Paul? I thought he was coming."

April pushed out her bottom lip, tilted her head, and shrugged. "He—had an emergency of some sort. He sent me a text saying he would see us later."

Mutzi opened one of the bottles of wine. "Your wedding is getting close. Are you excited?"

"There's still a lot to do." April rolled her eyes. Truth was, the simple ceremony she wanted had manifested into a spectacle. Between her future in-laws' expectations and her own mother's extravagant taste, it no longer felt like her wedding. Deflecting the attention, April changed the subject. "So, how was the festival?"

"It went very well. And Mutzi did wonderful with her delightful gold bricks. They were a big hit." Marge smiled at her sister who poured wine into the goblets.

"Hmpf." Mutzi stuck a cork into the bottle and set it aside. "Glad it's over."

The response brought another frown from Marge. April bit her bottom lip. She glanced at her phone again, hoping for another text from Paul. When she looked up, both aunts were shaking their heads.

"Sorry. I'm frustrated that Paul hasn't answered me." She set the phone down and sighed.

Marge led them in a prayer and they began passing dishes in deafening silence.

April decided to break the ice. "I guess the Woman's Club is already working on the Christmas Market. Mom coming in town that week. I'm looking forward to seeing her."

"It'll be here before you know it. I'm going to have to start planning the menu for our dinner, too." Marge glanced toward the ceiling as if she were already making the grocery list.

April lifted her wine and offered a toast. "Here's to a delicious meal and a wonderful season ahead."

Marge lifted her glass. "To a joyful holiday."

Mutzi muttered, "With no more *accidents*."

Chapter Seven

April returned to her apartment well after dark, still concerned she'd heard nothing from Paul since his earlier text. The quiet residence felt empty without him. Turning on the news, she plopped down on the supple leather sofa, her stomach full from too much turkey, dressing, and pie.

Something in her pocket poked her leg. She reached in and pulled out Aunt Marge's unique ring, slipping it on her finger. With her hand under a nearby lamp, she studied the opal back-ground and the miniscule man panning for gold. The television droned in the background unnoticed until someone mentioned April's favorite restaurant.

"The Sun Dial, located at the Westin Hotel, is one of the few establishments open on Thanksgiving." The cameraman scanned across the entrance where a few patrons entered the building as a couple exited. The reporter hurried to their side. "How was your meal tonight?"

April's eyes were drawn to a tall, attractive man with nougat-brown hair who wore a sharp gray suit. He wrapped an arm around a curvy blonde whose long golden locks spilled over the collar of a herring-bone coat.

She jumped to her feet, eyes bulging and mouth agape, and screamed at the screen. "What the hell?" There was no mistaking. Her fiancé snuggled close to her best friend, Priscilla. She pressed the palms of her hands to her eyes to block the image from her mind. When she removed them, the station had gone to commercial.

She grabbed the remote and flipped channels trying to find them on another station. Unsuccessful, she jabbed the off button and threw the remote across the room just missing the television. "You son of bitch...how could you?" she shouted to the four walls, her heart pounding so hard she bent over and clutched her chest, struggling for air.

All the qualities April admired about her fiancé disintegrated into rubbish. Strong morals, honesty, integrity—gone. Angry tears streamed down her face.

They'd planned out the rest of their lives—a June wedding in the making and house hunting already underway. In two years, they'd have the first of three children. A ten second flash on the news shattered her dreams of marriage and ended a friendship she thought was invincible.

Priscilla Montgomery, the girl voted most likely to succeed in their graduating class, and April's life-long friend, cheating with her fiancé. Inseparable since the age of five, nothing could come between them. They'd supported one another through each of their parents' divorces, nurtured each other through high school, and encouraged each other to complete challenging college programs. The betrayal ripped at her heart.

She grabbed the car keys and flew out the door, refusing to be in the apartment when Paul came home. He'd make some lame excuse about where he'd been. No, if Priscilla wanted the two-timing jerk, she could have him. With no destination in mind, she drove the winding mountain roads, gripping the steering wheel and pressing harder on the gas.

A massive buck appeared in her headlights as April steered around a sharp curve, leaving no time to brake. She swerved, and the car careened off the unforgiving shoulder. Unbelted, April hit the windshield like a tossed rag doll. A loud hum filled her head as the lights went out around her.

When April regained consciousness, the pain stabbing at her neck reminded her of the turbulent jaunt. She sat motionless, afraid to move, and assessed the situation. The airbag on the passenger side had deployed when the animal impacted the front right fender. By some miracle, the car had not rolled. One by one, she checked her joints. First one wrist, then the other. A tinge of bruising formed on her left hand. She pried the rings off her swollen fingers and tucked them into her pocket.

Next, she tried to move one ankle, and then another. Her right knee hurt the worst. Stretching across the seat to retrieve her cellphone from the floor mat where it had landed, an intense stabbing in her ribcage brought a high-pitched scream. After a few deep breaths, she tried again. Her fingertips inched the phone closer until it was within reach.

Out of habit, she pressed one on her speed dial. A flashback to the news report made her hang up before Paul answered. She closed her eyes and sucked in another breath. The excruciating pain in her midsection grew strong as she pressed 911. The phone slipped from her hand as she lost consciousness again.

April faded in and out as emergency responders removed her from the wreckage. By the time they delivered her to the emergency room in Gainesville, she didn't care if she lived or died. Without Paul in her life, it wasn't worth living.

During the next few hours, she endured the gruesome cleaning of her wounds, x-rays and lab tests, silently hoping the end would come soon. Her hair matted to her face from the constant tears she shed.

A doctor pulled back the curtain and neared her bedside, while a nurse stood near the IV and checked its drip. "Ms. Preston, I'm Doctor Tucker. How's your pain?"

April tried to scoot up in the bed and winced in pain. "I feel like I got ran over by a Mack truck."

"The tests show you've got a broken rib, numerous contusions, and a slight concussion. You're going to be quite sore for a while, but you're very fortunate."

She knew she should be grateful. Her bruised ribs, wrist and knee would heal in time. But no one mentioned the condition of her broken heart. April sighed. "Thanks."

"We're going to keep you until morning to monitor the concussion. Any questions?"

The only thought that came to mind couldn't be answered by the doctor. "No."

"Make sure to take it easy for the next few days. The nurse will give you instructions. Follow up with your primary within the week." He nodded his head and left the room.

The nurse remained and adjusted April's pillow. "Can I get you something to eat or drink?"

"Where's my phone?"

The nurse on duty retrieved a plastic bag from a

hook and handed it to April. "We couldn't find a phone. This is all they brought in with you."

April closed her eyes and gnawed on her bottom lip. "No phone. No car. No fiancée." She clenched her arms against her chest and sobbed.

The nurse grabbed a few tissues and handed them to April. "Can I call someone for you?"

"I guess. My aunts live in Dahlonega. I hate to bother them, but I don't have anyone else." She provided the nurse with their number. "Tell them not to come until tomorrow and ask them not to tell anyone."

The nurse pulled the curtain closed as she left the room. "Try to sleep for a while."

The suggestion came as a relief. April closed her eyes. Before long, she drifted into a restless slumber.

Marge and Mutzi burst into the hospital room the following morning, waking April with a startle.

"We've been calling and calling, trying to reach you." Marge's eyes grew wide and her hands flew to her cheeks. "Oh my, oh dear. You're all bruised. You poor thing. How'd this happen?"

April reached to touch her forehead. "Deer versus car. I lost."

Mutzi stepped closer, examining the raised bandage wrapped around April's head. "Looks like that's a nasty bump. Gonna leave a mark."

"X-rays didn't show anything upstairs except a slight concussion."

Mutzi flashed a grin at her niece. "Keep that sense of humor, girl. Comes in handy on days like this."

Reaching for April's hand, Marge tilted her head and asked, "What in the world were you doing out so late? Paul called looking for you. He's worried sick, but I didn't tell him, like you asked."

April glanced away before responding. "Paul doesn't need to know where I am."

The two sisters stared at each and then refocused on April. "What's going on?" they asked as one.

"I don't want to talk about it." April motioned for her clothes. "Maybe later."

Marge pulled the curtain closed. "Let's get you out of here. You can stay with us for a few days until you feel better."

"It may be longer than that," April muttered to herself.

"I think you should let Paul know you're all right."

April's eyes brimmed with moisture. "Paul's seeing Priscilla." Her face flushed as tears streamed down her cheeks. "The engagement's off. My internship with the firm is gone, and so is my car. How's that for a happy Thanksgiving?"

Chapter Eight

Stirred from sleep by a nightmare, Mutzi tossed the covers aside and sat straight up. Images of April slipping the gold miner ring on her finger flashed across her mind. Why would she dream that? April didn't even know about the ring. In fact, Mutzi hadn't seen the ring since Thanksgiving.

Fear settled in her belly, causing it to ache. Had the dream been a vision? A premonition? She couldn't take the chance. There had to be a way to stop the curse before the ring did any more damage. She threw on a robe and hurried into the kitchen to make a pot of coffee. When the pot finished brewing, she poured a cup and wandered outside to the front porch swing.

Why did Marge have to buy that damn brick? She wanted to blame her sister, yet, she knew it was not her fault. If she hadn't taken it to begin with—it shamed her to think about what she'd done. She didn't want to talk with Marge about it. But now what could she do?

Perhaps the curse rejuvenated itself when she removed it from the hidden place in her drawer. When

Mutzi first experienced its repercussions, she'd focused on neutralizing the contaminated ring. She'd followed the suggestions found on the internet for breaking a cursed object. She purified the jewelry in holy water and prayed for it to be cleansed. Unsure if the procedure worked, she'd stashed it away.

April's accident weighed heavy on Mutzi. She couldn't connect the dots, but her gut told her there was more to it than she knew.

Marge appeared at the front door, breaking the vicious thought cycle. "Couldn't sleep?"

"Na." Mutzi stared off, her empty cup bobbing in her lap.

"Mind if I join you?"

Mutzi motioned to the rocker. "Have at it."

Her sister sat down. They rocked for a little while without speaking, the ring continued to consume Mutzi's attention.

"Looks like you're doing some heavy thinking."

Mutzi fiddled with the cup. "How can you be so sure about everything? Like hexes and curses?"

"That's a strange thing to ask first thing in the morning." Marge leaned forward and stopped the motion of the swing. "What's on your mind?"

Mutzi reconsidered and decided not to pursue the conversation. "Never mind."

"One of your superstitions bothering you?" Marge

chuckled. "You know I don't believe in all that black cat and walking under a ladder nonsense."

"Forget it." Mutzi shot up from her rocker and stormed inside.

Marge followed her. "How about some breakfast? I think April's coming down soon. I'll make us some pancakes and bacon. Get your mind off whatever's bothering you."

Mutzi shrugged her shoulders and refilled her cup.

April limped into the kitchen, her knee wrapped in an elastic bandage. "Morning." The dark circles under her eyes made it clear she'd had a rough night.

Marge pulled out a chair for her niece. "We can stop by the drug store and get you a pair of crutches today."

Leaning her arm on the island, April cradled her head in one hand. "I'll be fine. Just a little bruised knee...and fractured rib...and a broken heart."

Mutzi picked up the carafe. "Coffee?"

"I'd rather have tea, if you don't mind."

"I'll put the kettle on."

"What'd you decide about work on Monday? Did you call and tell them about the accident?"

"They probably already know. The gossip mill spreads pretty fast." She shifted in her chair. "I don't know if I can go back there. Seeing Paul every day would kill me."

Marge tilted her head and looked at April. "I can't believe he cheated on you. You're sure that's what happened? I think you should talk to him before calling it quits."

April's face reddened and her eyes bulged. "I saw him on television with his arm wrapped around Priscilla. Didn't look like any *emergency* to me."

"Men." Mutzi shook her head. "They can't be trusted."

"Mutzi. Don't say that. It's not true. My George—"

"Your George was one of a kind. Most men are fools."

"Enough of that talk." Marge layered the bacon on a cookie sheet and put it in the oven. Grabbing a box of mix from the cupboard, she asked, "How many pancakes do you want?"

Mutzi held up two fingers in response.

April thought for a moment. "I'll take three."

Mutzi paced back and forth, her mind still racing. She needed to get the ring back from Marge without revealing why. "Do you have a meeting this week, Marge?"

Marge handed the syrup and butter to Mutzi to set on the island. "Not until Wednesday. We rescheduled the tour of Gibbs Gardens. Why do you ask?"

"Just wondering." Mutzi scrunched her face, working on a plan. She needed Marge out of the house to make it happen.

Mutzi wandered back and forth while Marge flipped the pancakes and April buried her head in a magazine. When the timer dinged, Marge took the bacon out of the oven and distributed it evenly on three dishes along with the requested pancakes.

She handed Mutzi one of the plates. Without thinking, Mutzi sat down and started eating.

"You might want to wait until we all get seated," Marge snapped.

Mutzi dropped her fork and looked up at her sister. "Sorry. I—didn't mean to be rude. Got something on my mind."

April reached across the table and placed her hand on Mutzi's arm. "Want to talk about it?"

"Na. I'll work it out. You've got enough on your mind."

Marge spoke without looking at her sister. "If you don't want to talk with us about it, maybe you should run it by the reverend. He's good at listening."

April's eyes widened with the suggestion, and her eyes darted to Mutzi. "I didn't know you rejoined the church?"

Mutzi picked up her fork, flipping it around as she thought. "I haven't. But, it's not a bad idea." She pressed her lips tight and let out a sigh as she stared at Marge. "Maybe I will."

Conversations ceased, emphasizing the sound of scraping forks and knives on plates. Seemed everyone had something on their mind, but kept it to themselves.

April broke the silence. "I've heard Gibbs Gardens is amazing."

Marge nodded. "It is. They have a number of fall festivals and other activities for Christmas. My favorite time is in the spring when the azaleas and daffodils are blooming. They have a Monet Waterlily Garden that is just magnificent."

"Sounds like a great venue for taking wedding pictures." April sighed and dropped her napkin on the table. "Too bad mine's cancelled."

"Oh April. Don't say that. Give Paul a chance to explain." Marge pleaded with her eyes.

April pushed her chair away. "I don't think there's anything he could say that would make me change my mind."

Marge ran some hot soapy water and began washing the dishes while Mutzi dried them. When the dishes were finished, Mutzi went outside. She walked down the street to the church and went inside the rectory.

Reverend Mitch greeted her with a broad smile. "Well, fancy seeing you here, Miss McGilvray."

"Got a few minutes?"

"Of course. What seems to be troubling you?" The reverend motioned for her to take a seat.

"Not sure where to start." She drew in a deep breath and muttered, "That's not true. I know where to start, but I'm avoiding it."

"You're safe here, Mutzi. Whatever you tell me, we'll work it out, together."

"If you take something that doesn't rightfully belong to you..." Mutzi paused trying to decide how to word her question.

"Did you...steal something?"

"It wasn't really stealing." She took another deep breath and exhaled. "Maybe it was. It was a long time ago. When I was teenager."

"And this thing is still bothering you today?"

"It's hard to explain." She squirmed in her chair, wanting to get up and walk around. Forcing herself to sit, she wrung her hands on her lap. "My father," Mutzi's voice softened like a child as she spoke, "he always liked my oldest sister best. Anyone could tell. She was the prettiest and she always got the best gifts, adult things. Things I wanted."

The reverend leaned forward and nodded.

"My father often brought us gifts. Think he tried to compensate for our mother passing away." Mutzi hung her head for a moment. "He traveled a lot. One time, I was the only one home and he was leaving for another trip. He handed me three boxes. The one wrapped in pink paper was for me, a red one for Marge—that's her favorite color—and the blue one was for Rose Ellen. He told me to give my sisters theirs when they got home." Mutzi swallowed hard. "I kept the blue one for myself and gave the pink one to Rose Ellen."

"And you never told her?"

"No." Mutzi stood and began pacing. "It was a ring. I took it and it didn't belong to me. Then bad things started happening."

"What kind of bad things?"

"First it was little things, like the needle on my record player broke and scratched my favorite 45. It was our song, Sam's and mine." Tears threatened to spill from her eyes and she brushed them away.

"Then I failed a test, which I know I should have passed. It resulted in me losing a scholarship. Without tuition, I couldn't go to college." She drew in a deep breath. "I should have aced that test."

The reverend rested his hand on his chin. "That was unfortunate."

"Then my dad got sick. He thought it was just a cold. It turned out to be pneumonia." Mutzi choked out the words, "And he died."

"And you think you were to blame?"

"I think God hates me. He was mad at me for taking something that wasn't mine."

The reverend met Mutzi's eyes. "God doesn't work that way, Mutzi."

"But it didn't stop. First my dad, then Sam."

"Tell me about Sam."

"Samuel Parks. The best friend I ever had." She no longer fought back the tears. They trailed down her cheeks. "I loved him. We were going to get married when he came back from Vietnam. I wrote to him every day. And he always wrote back."

Mutzi reached for a tissue on the corner of the reverend's desk and dabbed at her eyes. "After I wrote to him about my dad and told him about the ring, that was it. I never heard from him again. I must have killed him, too."

The reverend stood and walked over to Mutzi, patting her on the shoulder. "You've held onto these pains for a long time, Mutzi. I know things haven't been easy for you. But what's happened to bring all this to the surface now?"

Mutzi stopped pacing. The picture she'd found in a box of old photos Marge stored in a closet flashed through her mind. Mutzi had no idea who had taken the picture, but the fact she was positioned between Marge and Rose Ellen freaked her out. Stories on the internet predicted the sibling in the middle would be the first to die, and Mutzi believed them.

If she told the pastor the reason she needed to get rid of the ring, would he believe her or deny her fear as a superstition, just like Marge would do? But, maybe he could help her figure out what to do with the ring.

"I tried to give the ring away, but Marge ended up with it. Now bad things are happening to her." Mutzi pulled another tissue from the box and blew her nose. "The ring is cursed."

"I'm not sure the ring has anything to do with all of this, but let's explore a possible solution. What do you think would be the right thing to do?"

Mutzi crossed her arms and frowned. "I don't know. That's why I'm here."

"I think you know the answer. You have unfinished business to attend to."

"But Marge has the ring. I'd have to tell her that I stole it and I can't do that."

"Why not?"

Mutzi started pacing again. "You don't understand. Marge does everything right. She's probably never committed a sin in her life. She's right in line for sainthood."

"No one's perfect, Mutzi."

"She's about as close as you can come. If I tell her, she'll be mad at me. Maybe mad enough to kick me out on the street."

"I've known Marge for some time. I don't think she'd do that. Especially since it happened so long ago."

"What if I got it back from her, without her knowing, and brought it to you. Could you bless it? Maybe that would get rid of the evil spirits. I've read about things being un-blessed."

"Wouldn't that be stealing it, again? Think about it. What do you really think is the right thing to do?"

Mutzi stared at the reverend. "I need to give it back to Rose Ellen." She swallowed hard. "And tell both of them the truth."

Reverend Mitch nodded. "It won't be easy, but you will feel better after you do."

She pulled her shoulders tight, the weight of reality hung heavy, making them ache. "I guess. I'll think about it."

"You've been thinking about it long enough."

Mutzi walked to the door and placed her hand on the knob. "Will God forgive me?"

"He already has. You need to forgive yourself."

Chapter Nine

Wednesday morning the sun shone bright through the window, bringing a smile to Mutzi's face. Good weather meant Marge's day outing wouldn't be cancelled. Sitting on the edge of her bed, she bounced her leg up and down waiting for her sister to leave the house. With her bedroom door ajar, she watched Marge slip on her burgundy wrap, then glance in the mirror to check her hair and makeup. *Enough. It's perfect, like always.*

"I'm leaving, Mutzi," she called out. "By the way, April decided to go to work today. You're on your own."

With that announcement, Mutzi jumped off the bed and hurried down the hall into the foyer. "Enjoy the gardens. The weatherman said it should be about 65 degrees, just right for walking around that huge Gibb's estate."

"I've left some chicken salad for you in the fridge. Croissants and chips are in the pantry."

"Sounds yummy. Thanks." Mutzi opened the door and waited as Marge took one last glance in the mirror. "You better get going or you'll be late."

The side glance her sister sent came with a puzzled

look. "Are you in a hurry to get rid of me?"

Mutzi flushed warm at the suggestion. "You bet. I'll have the house all to myself. Who knows what I'll do." She wiggled her brows and added a devilish grin.

Marge shook her head. "You're so silly. Have a good day."

After the car backed out of the driveway and disappeared from view, Mutzi began her clandestine mission. The reverend said she needed to give the ring back to Rose Ellen, but did it really matter how she did it? The decision to mail it with a brief note had come to Mutzi as she tried to sleep the night before. First things first. She'd have to find it.

It had been some time since Mutzi had been in her sister's bedroom. It resembled a page from a decorating magazine. The half-dozen assorted pillows on the bed complimented the floral comforter and crisp drapes. Unlike her own cluttered room, where every surface held papers or books, Marge's oak nightstand and dresser glistened, not a hint of dust to be found. Disturbing the immaculate setting made Mutzi hesitate, but she needed to find that evil ring.

Marge's four-tiered jewelry box sat next to an ornate necklace tree, meticulously organized by chain length. Mutzi opened the bottom tray which contained watches and bracelets. The second had an assortment of broaches and the third was filled with earrings. The last one held a selection of rings: colorful ruby, sapphire and diamonds, but not the gold miner ring.

"Crap. Where the heck did she put it?" Mutzi fussed as she extended her search into a dresser drawer.

"What are you doing in here?"

Startled by the unexpected voice, Mutzi jumped and knocked over the box, catching it before it crashed, but flinging jewelry onto the floor. "Damn it!"

Marge stood in the doorway, her hands on her hips. "I've warned you before. None of that language in this house."

"I know. I know." Mutzi scrambled to pick up the fallen items. "You scared the sh—stuffing out of me."

"*I* startled *you*? I certainly didn't expect to find you digging through my drawers. What are you looking for?"

Their eyes locked. Mutzi cleared her throat. "I...need the ring back."

"What?"

"The one that was in the brick."

Marge grabbed the jewelry box from Mutzi and set it on the dresser. "You can stop looking for it. I don't have it."

Her mouth agape, Mutzi reached out and grabbed

her sister's arm. "Where is it?"

Marge yanked her arm away and smoothed her wrap. "I gave it to April. She admired it and I knew something about it upset you, so I gave it to her."

The words sent Mutzi to her knees, clenching her chest. "Oh, my God. When? When did you give it to her?"

Marge bent down, facing her sister. "For Heaven's sake. Are you okay? What's wrong, Mutzi?"

Mutzi sucked in air and exhaled. "When?"

"I gave it to her while we were doing dishes on Thanksgiving. I thought it would make things better between us."

Mutzi's stomach churned at the thought of yet another person being involved in her mess. "But it made things worse—for April. Look what's happened to her."

Marge pressed her lips tight and shook her head. "Mutzi, the ring didn't make those things happen."

Mutzi held onto the dresser as she struggled to stand. "You'll never understand."

"Understand what, Sis. Tell me."

She couldn't force the words from her mouth. "You're going to be late. Why'd you come back?"

"I forgot my watch." Marge reached past her sister and removed the silver watch from her dresser top. "You're sure you don't need me to stay?"

"No." She released her grip from the dresser. "Go. It's my mess. I'm the only one to fix it."

"We'll talk about this when I get home." Marge brushed her sister's hair away from her eyes, and sighed. "Please put this stuff back where you found it."

Mutzi wrung her hands. "Marge, I'm sorry. I really am, for causing you so many problems. Please don't hate me."

"For Heaven's sake. I don't hate you." She touched Mutzi's cheek. "You fluster me sometimes. But I could never hate you."

Mutzi hoped it was true. She hugged Marge and urged her to be on her way. After returning everything to the jewelry box the best she could, she went to her own room and collapsed on the bed. The overwhelming feeling of failure exhausted her. Even her plan to avoid telling everyone what she did years ago had fallen apart. Maybe Reverend Mitch was right. She'd have to confess her indiscretion, and face the consequences. And it had to be soon, before any more disasters occurred.

Chapter Ten

*A*pril unlocked the door to the law firm and made her way into her office. She flipped on the lights and sat down at her desk, mentally prioritizing a list of things she needed to do. She double-checked the calendar, confirming Paul was due in court. Hopefully, he wouldn't come into the office before or after the hearing.

Another intern showed up within the hour and poked her head in April's office. "Hi. Glad to see you're back. How are you feeling?"

"A little sore, but not bad." April stood and picked up a notebook, hoping to limit the conversation. "I need to do some research. Going to bury myself in the giant tomes."

"Paul's been asking about you."

April turned away from the woman as if she didn't hear her. She had no intention of discussing the situation with this woman, much less Paul. She excused herself and walked out, for once grateful to escape to the library.

Often, her work provided little excitement and involved go-for tasks. Go for coffee, go for lunch, and go for copies of this and that. But recently, she'd been asked to research background documents to support an upcoming trial, a sign they were beginning to take her skills and abilities more seriously. What a shame she might have to leave.

Working through lunch, April didn't return to her office until late afternoon. She shut down her computer and organized her folders before stuffing them in a drawer for the next day. With a blank piece of paper in hand, she listed tasks to tackle in the morning.

A knock on her door made her look up to find Paul standing there in his light gray suit, the one with the structured silhouette that accented his near-perfect body. His wavy brown hair dangled slightly above well-manicured brows and those enticing chocolate eyes. Her heart beat faster, just as it had every time she laid eyes on him.

A flashback of him hugging Priscilla dissipated the tender moment. Steam permeated her body, like ice water on a fire. She refocused her eyes on the unfinished list.

"April. What's going on?" He stepped closer. "You haven't returned my calls. I've been worried about you."

Daggers shot from her eyes to his. "You cheated on me with my best friend."

Paul's head jerked back, his brows drawn tight forming a crease. "What are you talking about? I'd never—"

April slammed the pad onto the desk. "I saw you with my own eyes, on the news." She glared at Paul. "Thanksgiving, when you had an *emergency*." Slinging her purse over her shoulder, she tried to walk past him.

Paul shook his head and stepped into her path, blocking her from leaving. "You're wrong. It's not what you think." He reached out and held her shoulders. "I...please, let me explain.

She tried to ignore the warmth of his touch. How could she continue to work in the same office with Paul? The thought of seeing him every day terrified her. Not seeing him devastated her more. "There's nothing you could say to erase what I saw. Goodbye, Paul."

He tipped his head and sighed. "You're right. I was with Priscilla on Thanksgiving. I—"

Raising her hands to Paul's chest, she pushed him back. "I don't want to hear your excuse." She slipped her engagement ring off her finger and thrust it at him. "We're done."

His cheeks burned bright red. "April...I love you and I know you love me. Don't do this."

The desk phone rang, and she pointed to the door. "Leave. Now." She picked up the receiver and turned her back to him. "Crofton, Brown and Williams. How may I help you?" She turned around as Paul disappeared from sight and she heard the door close. The weight of what she'd done sent sharp pains through her chest like a knife cutting out her heart. She finished the call and turned out the lights.

The sun faded into the horizon as she approached her rental car. April set her purse on the trunk and searched for her keys. The ring Marge had given her caught her eye and she slipped it on her finger. Next she pulled out her wallet, a package of tissues, some hand cream, and eye drops, but no keys. Bending down, she peered through the car window and saw the missing items dangling from the steering wheel. "Shit!" Her voice echoed across the empty lot.

The newly purchased cell phone shook in April's hand as she dialed for road service.

"Can you hold, please?"

The woman put her on hold before April could say no. She fumed and stomped her foot, sending shooting pain through her not-yet-mended knee. Tears pooled in her eyes, but she refused to let them fall.

The woman's voice returned. "How can I help you?"

"I've locked my keys in the car." While April gave the receptionist the address, a gust of wind scattered half of the items from her purse across the parking lot. She cursed again as she scrambled to retrieve them, still holding the phone to her ear.

"I'm sorry, miss. Ten minutes is the best we can do."

"Sorry. I wasn't cursing at you. Ten minutes is fine. Great."

By the time April retrieved and stashed the things back into her purse, the tow truck driver arrived.

Using a tool, the young man unlocked the door and pulled it open. "You might want to get an extra key made."

"Wish I'd thought of that." April wrinkled her nose and handed him a tip.

The normal twenty-minute drive to Dahlonega took an hour due to heavy traffic and an accident at one of the busiest intersections. Supper was on the table when she limped into her aunt's kitchen.

Marge looked up at April. "Running a little late tonight? You must have been busy catching up on things."

"Paul came by and I broke up with him." She sucked in a deep breath and released it. "Then I locked my keys in the car. And to top it off, there was an accident on 400. At least this time I wasn't in it. Another wonderful day in the life of April Preston."

She reached across the table and picked up a dinner roll. The gold ring flashed under the ceiling light.

Mutzi grabbed her napkin in time to catch the water that shot from her mouth.

Marge's eyes met her sister's and she shook her head no.

April looked from one aunt to the other. "What's going on, you two?"

"We'll talk about it later, dear. Let's have a relaxing dinner first," Marge replied.

Pulling a chair out, April slumped into it. "Let's talk about it now."

Each aunt gazed at the other, appearing to wait for the other to begin. Finally, Marge cleared her throat. "Aunt Mutzi has some concerns—superstitions about your difficult week."

"They aren't superstitions, Marge. You know that. I'm not delusional," Mutzi spouted back.

"I didn't say you were delusional."

April dropped the roll onto her plate and shouted, "Just tell me."

Neither sister moved. April placed her hands over her eyes for a moment and then dropped them. "I'm sorry. My patience is frayed."

Mutzi put down her napkin. "It's the ring. The one Marge gave you." She bit her lip as she stared at the ring in question. "I need you to give it back to me."

"All right." April slipped the ring off her finger. "Now tell me what's going on."

"I hate this." Mutzi sucked in a deep breath and released it. "The ring is cursed. Bad things happen to whoever wears it."

Marge let out a groan. "Such nonsense. And it's whomever."

April ignored Marge and turned her body toward Mutzi. "What kind of things?"

"Marge gave you the ring on Thanksgiving. Look at all the things that have gone wrong for you since then. I bet you were wearing it when you saw Paul with Priscilla... and when you wrecked your car. You were wearing it today and look what happened."

April looked up trying to remember. "I *was* wearing it that evening. But what makes you think the ring had anything to do with all those things?"

"When Marge had it, she got a flat tire, her expensive new purse broke, and she sprained her ankle, all in the same day. I'm telling you, it's hexed."

Marge grumbled, "You still haven't told me where you got the ring, Mutzi."

Mutzi met her sister's stare.

"The ring doesn't belong to me. Never did." Mutzi turned her attention to April. "It was meant for your mother."

Marge's eyes widened. "Rose Ellen?" She slammed her hand on the table. "Did you go through *her* jewelry box, too?"

Mutzi jerked back as if she'd been slapped. Her eyes brimmed with tears. "No. Of course not." She stood and began wandering back and forth.

"Remember the time Daddy came home late from the Gold Rush Festival and brought all of us gifts. You and Rose Ellen were out on dates. He went to bed early because he was leaving the next morning for a trip. He gave me the boxes to give to each of you."

Marge reached out and stopped Mutzi from circling the table again. "And..."

"Rose Ellen always got the best gifts. She was his favorite."

"Stop that, Mutzi. It's not true. She was older and—never mind. Go on with your story."

"I gave Rose Ellen the box meant for me. I took hers. It was the ring."

Marge stared at the ring. "But I've never seen you wear it."

"I was too embarrassed. I put it on when I was in my room, but I only wore it out when I was sure neither of you would see it."

"That's crazy. Why bother stealing it? Shame on you."

April scowled at Marge. "Let her finish." She placed a hand on Mutzi's arm. "What bad things happened to *you* when you had it?"

Marge grunted. "Don't encourage her, April."

"Little things at first. The chain on a necklace my boyfriend gave me broke. Our favorite 45 got scratched." Mutzi took a breath. "Then I flunked an algebra test and lost a scholarship to college."

"You didn't want to go to college anyway," Marge fussed.

Mutzi ignored her remark. "Two days later, Sam got orders for Vietnam."

Marge persisted. "Lots of boys got called to go there."

Mutzi's jaw harden and her cheeks turn scarlet red.

"The next time I wore it, Daddy got sick. Then he died." She covered her face with both hands and sobbed.

April had never seen her aunt cry. She sat in silence, unsure what to say or do.

The emotional response softened Marge's face. "Oh, Mutzi, that wasn't because of the ring."

When Mutzi regained her composure, she added, "No. It wasn't the ring. God punished me for taking what wasn't mine. He took Daddy."

April and Marge spoke at the same time. "It wasn't your fault he died."

Mutzi shook her head. "I wrote to Sam and told him what I did. I never heard from him again. We were supposed to be married. I love him." Her body shook. "Maybe he died too. Maybe I killed him." She wailed as if her heart tore in two.

Marge jumped up from her chair and wrapped her arms around her sister, stroking her hair. "Honey, I'm sorry. I didn't realize you carried these thoughts all these years. I didn't know."

After a few minutes, Mutzi looked up at Marge. "I think that's enough proof that it's cursed. Don't you?"

"No, honey. I don't think all those things happened because of the ring, or as punishment. God doesn't work that way."

Mutzi sank into a chair. "I wish I believed that." She choked back more sobs. "Reverend Mitch says I need to give the ring back to Rose Ellen. That's why I was looking in your jewelry box. I wanted to do the right thing and send it to her."

"It's alright. I understand now." Marge took her sister's hands in hers. "We'll make this right. I'll help you."

April smiled at her aunt. "Mom will be here in a few days. You can give her the ring then. Knowing her, she'll dismiss the whole thing as a silly mistake. Then you'll be done with it, whether it's cursed or not."

Marge pulled a chair up close to her sister. "You still love Sam, don't you?"

Mutzi nodded. "Always have, always will."

Chapter Eleven

*O*ther than the evergreens, most of the trees on the rural roads from Virginia to Georgia were bare. The eleven hour drive took its toll on Sam's aging body. He rolled his shoulders and twisted his neck as he slowed the truck and pulled onto the six acres surrounding the well-kept ranch home where he'd grown up.

Water trickled across the rocky creek bed that edged its way around both sides of the house, flowing into the small pond near the corner of the property. The rustic remains of the century-old, twenty-foot tall fireplace still towered on the right, a reminder of where the original lodge once stood more than a hundred years earlier.

A rush of childhood memories made him smile. The eighty-year-old towering walnut tree near the front of the house shed its fruit on the sidewalk. He kicked one into the air like he'd done a million times before.

Two wooden rockers his father built when Sam was a mere lad enhanced the large wrap-around porch. He settled onto one and swayed to the sound of cicada humming in the massive oaks.

Ah, Mutzi. We sat right here and studied the stars while exploring what our life together would be when I returned from Nam. They'd spoken of children, lots of children, laughing and playing tag between the trees, even picked out names.

The sting of reality wiped away his smile. The damn war shot down those dreams. Sent them both on different journeys. Here he was, holding onto a piece of the dream, the piece where they grew old together. Who was he to think their love could resurrect?

Leaving her the way he had seemed the right thing to do. Even though he did it to free her, he'd hurt her deeply—that he knew without hearing it from Mutzi. Circumstances forced his youthful decision. Maybe they weren't meant to be. Still, he regretted the pain he'd caused the woman he loved. *Could she ever understand? Could she forgive me?*

Sam stopped rocking and stood, ready to enter his childhood home. He retrieved the key from under the doormat. Most folks in the area never locked a door, but the realty company had insisted.

Neighbors kept an eye on everything and everyone. While it meant things were safe, it also meant there were few, if any, secrets. If the Smiths had company from out of town, in less than an hour, everyone knew their names and from where they came. A repair truck in the driveway indicated the Jones' refrigerator was on the blink again.

The transparency didn't bother Sam. He had nothing to hide, though he knew his return would stir gossip. Once his story was told, he hoped things would settle down.

It took a few hours to unload the truck and put things in their rightful place. Most of the furniture had been left by the previous owner, a friend of the family who'd bought the house and its contents when Sam's parents died. Now that man was gone and his family, who'd inherited it, had no use for the relics Sam treasured.

Though he'd had months to prepare, the thought of seeing Mutzi again made his nerves twitch and his empty belly churn. He'd tried to envision their first meeting and what words he'd choose to beg her forgiveness.

The more he planned, the worse his fears grew. Once he stepped foot into town, word of his return would spread faster than butter on hot bread. He wondered how long it would be before he ran into her.

Procrastinating, Sam made a list of items he'd need from the local hardware store. After that, he'd stop at the food market to stock up on staples and a few cuts of meat. The thought of a warm, juicy sandwich made his stomach rumble. Postponing the inevitable was no longer an option. He needed something to eat soon, not a few hours from now.

It took two trips around the town square before Sam found a parking spot near the Dahlonega Gold Museum, across the street from Shenanigan's Irish Pub. He wet his lips in anticipation of a cold beer and a hearty sandwich. Perhaps his empty stomach would stop growling. He'd skipped many meals during the past few months, having little appetite and no one to cook for. Something about the clean, crisp air brought back his appetite with a vengeance.

As soon as he walked in the door Sam recognized the bartender, an old high school friend. The man glanced up, squinted his eyes and shook his head as Sam moved closer.

"Well, don't that beat all? Sam Parks. Thought you died in Nam." He extended his hand for a shake.

"Almost did." Sam nodded toward the ceiling. "Guess the man up there had other plans for me. How you doing, Joe?"

"Can't complain. Still kicking." He grabbed a glass from the cooler. "Whatcha drinking?"

Sam planted himself on a stool by the bar. "Got a pale ale?"

Joe filled the frosty mug to the top, being careful

not to leave a head. "So where've you been all this time?"

"Long story. But I'm back now. Plan on staying rooted here until it's my time."

"Heard your dad's place is up for sale."

"Not any more. Closed on it last week and moved in today."

The bartender's cheek rose to a half smile. "Well, I'll be. Ain't life funny?"

Sam bobbed his head. "Yep. Sure is." He picked up the two-sided menu and flipped it over. "How about grilling me a Reuben? Maybe some fries too?"

"Sure thing." Joe scribbled the order on a piece of paper and hit the bell on the counter signaling the cook. "Whatcha gonna do now that you're back in town?"

"Take some time to relax and then decide. I finally retired from the Army after thirty years. Did almost another twenty working at the Pentagon."

Joe rubbed his chin. "Not sure I'll ever be able to afford retirement." He picked up a rag and wiped a spill.

Sam turned toward the window. "Surprised to see the leather place still open. Who's running it?"

"Smith is. One tough dude." Joe stacked a few glasses, then tilted his head. "Ya know, there's quite a few of the folks still here. Either lots of good genes or healthy living in this part of the country."

"That's good." Sam sipped his beer. "Guess the gossip line's still active?"

"You bet. Wait until they get wind of your return. Speaking of which, whatever happened with you and that McGilvray girl—what's her name—Mugzi?"

Sam choked. He grabbed a napkin and wiped his face. "Mutzi." He gnawed on the inside of his mouth before answering. "Unfortunate circumstances, Joe."

"Shame. You two seemed destined to be together. Funny lady, always marches to her own drum, if you know what I mean. She never married. Still lives with her sister in that big old house."

The revelation stunned Sam. He tried to mask the hint of excitement that sparked and caused his heart to skip a beat. "Really?"

"Yup. Now her twin, Marge—she married a guy named George. He passed away a couple years ago. Nice fellow. He loved his beer."

"You don't say."

Joe placed a hefty plate of food in front of Sam. "Y'all by yourself?"

"All by myself." Sam focused on the corned beef and sauerkraut oozing out from the crisp grilled bread. The enticing aroma made Sam's stomach rumble as he bit into it. He finished chewing and took a sip of ale. "Haven't had anything this good since the wife passed away."

"Man that sucks. I lost mine to a heart attack last year. Awful quiet without her."

"Sorry to hear that, Joe."

Both men quieted with the solemn exchange. Sam finished his food and beer, and then paid his bill.

Joe reached across the counter for another handshake. "Glad you're back. Hope we see you around for a long time."

"Thanks. Not planning on going anywhere too soon."

Sam walked across the street to his truck and his eyes were drawn to Woody's Barber Shop next to the Georgia Wine and Oyster Bar. A banner in the front window announced its 90 year anniversary for servicing the men of the Military College of Georgia. Sam had received his first crew cut there as a child and again, right before he bid Mutzi goodbye and left for the Army. The bittersweet memory pained him.

Mutzi stuffed six books into her bag and headed down the street to the Conner Community Garden. Daisy mums, still in bloom, attracted dozens of vibrant butterflies near the fountain. She added the paperbacks to the small collection in the quaint "Take a book, Leave a book" miniature house that stood on a pedestal in the center of the garden. She decided to sit on a bench for a while, as she often did, reminiscing about the evenings she'd spent in this same place with Sam. The chill of the metal bench warmed as the sun beat on her. She closed her eyes and let her mind drift.

The mellow tone of a song echoing from the town square soothed her as she listened in silence. It was their song. Hers and Sam's. Had she imagined it? It sounded so close, so real. Mutzi opened her eyes a sliver, not wanting to disturb the moment, but curious to see if someone was near.

"Hello, Mutzi."

The familiar deep voice startled her and she jumped to her feet. "Sam?"

The man who stole her heart when she was just a teen. The man she dreamed of nearly every night. But, it couldn't be. He's dead. If not, it meant he'd abandoned her.

Mutzi faltered, her breath coming in sharp, quick gasps, her heart beating so hard surely it would burst. She turned to leave, to escape the turmoil racing in her head.

Sam reached to touch her arm, then hesitated. "Oh, Mutzi." He moved closer and his hands caressed her shoulders as he closed the distance between them.

Mutzi dared to look into his sky blue eyes. The anger and fear melted like paraffin on a hot stove. Years of longing for his warm embrace, to taste the sweetness of his lips, to wrap herself in the security of his presence, flooded her mind. She couldn't speak, say his name, nor chastise him for leaving.

With the tenderness of caressing a fallen bird, he pulled her closer and held her, whispering her name. She felt the beating of his heart, thumping hard like her own. The clean, woodsy scent of his aftershave filled her senses and she succumbed to the overwhelming need to respond. With trembling fingers, he lifted her chin and their lips touched, sending quivers through her aging body.

She pulled back, her eyes searching his weathered face for answers, unable to withdraw from the intimacy of the moment, sure it was only a dream.

He responded in a soothing, quiet murmur. "My love, my forever love."

The familiar words he'd muttered the last time they were together, stabbed at her chest. She pushed him away, her mind reeling as she hurried toward home, Sam calling her name as she climbed the steep hill to her sister's house. She didn't...couldn't...look back.

Chapter Twelve

*A*pril stood alongside the shiny new sedan she'd parked in the driveway and grinned as her aunt approached. She extended a hand in a Vanna White fashion toward the car as if making an introduction. "What do you think?"

Mutzi glanced at it and then climbed the steps of the porch. "Nice."

The modest response shocked April. "Are you all right?" She'd expected her aunt to demand to see all the latest gadgets and electronics equipped on the car. She loved those kind of things. Instead, the storm door slammed behind Mutzi without another word.

April hurried up the porch steps and went inside, searching for her aunt. The door to Mutzi's room shut so hard the pictures on the wall rattled. April followed the sound and tapped on the closed door. "Mutzi, what's wrong?" Silence filled the hallway. "Please, talk to me." She waited a few minutes. "Can I come in?" She turned the knob, not waiting for an answer and went inside.

Mutzi paced from one corner of the room to the other. "I—I don't believe it."

"What?" April stepped closer to her aunt and

placed a hand on her shoulder, trying to still her. "What don't you believe?"

"He's alive. He's back." Mutzi's eyes widened, her face bright red. "I should be happy, but I'm..."

"Who's back?" April struggled to understand.

Mutzi slowed for a moment and stared at April. "Sam. Sam Parks." She began pacing again.

April stepped in front of her aunt, and then patted the end of the bed, encouraging Mutzi to take a seat. "The man you once loved? How do you know?"

Mutzi's head swiveled toward the door, then back at April. "I was sitting on a bench, in the park, and he appeared out of nowhere. Then he kissed me." Verbalizing the situation sent Mutzi into motion again, she bounced up and tried to get past her niece.

Worried her aunt might hurt herself rushing around, or worse, have a heart attack, April took hold of Mutzi's hands and whispered, "Breathe. Take a slow, deep breath and relax." She mimicked the motion for her. "You're getting too worked up. Just breathe."

The soothing encouragement appeared to help. Mutzi sat back down on the bed. "I don't want Marge to know I kissed him."

"I won't tell. But, I think she'd understand. Don't you?" She searched her aunt's face for more information.

"How could she? *I* can't believe I did it." Mutzi whimpered like an injured pup. "All these years I waited for word from him, wondering what happened. Why'd he stop writing? Why didn't he come back for me like he promised?" She grabbed a tissue from the nightstand. "What if he's married? What if he never cared for me the way I did for him?" Her eyes stared out the window. "What if he does?"

Years of buried emotions spilled across Mutzi's face: fear, anger, confusion, love. April's breakup with Paul had been different, but she recognized the pain of loving someone so deeply and then losing them. She pulled Mutzi into her arms and cradled her as she wept.

A short time later, April heard the front door open, and Marge called from the foyer, "Mutzi, whose car's in the driveway?"

April released her hold on her aunt. "I'll go distract her while you splash some water on your face. Come down when you're ready."

With a nod, Mutzi turned and headed to the bathroom.

April bound down the stairs and greeted Marge who had made her way into the kitchen. "Isn't it a beauty?"

Marge stirred the chili simmering in the crockpot. "Very sporty. You'll have to take us for a ride in it later."

"Sure." The delightful scent of cumin drifted through the room. "Umm. That smells good. Want me to set the table?"

"Let's eat at the island." Marge found an onion in the cupboard and pulled out a chopping block. She pointed to the fridge. "There's some shredded cheese in there and a salad."

April busied herself with the table settings, keeping an eye out for Mutzi. When she appeared, April crossed the room and wrapped an arm around her, leading her to the kitchen. "Look who decided to join us."

Marge continued chopping. "Hey, Sis. When did you come in?"

Whatever Mutzi mumbled was inaudible. April tightened her hold and nodded, trying to reassure her.

The chopping stopped and Marge looked up. "You're upset. What's wrong?"

Mutzi opened her mouth as if she were going to speak and then pressed her lips tight. Her eyes darted to April, who nodded, urging her to continue. She tried again. "Sam. I saw Sam."

The knife dropped from Marge's hand and her eyes darted from Mutzi to April. "Sam Parks?"

April shrugged her shoulders and waited for Mutzi

to continue.

"Are you sure, Sis? Maybe you just saw someone who looked like him."

Mutzi hung her head, shaking it. "It was him."

The confirmation drew Marge nearer. She took Mutzi's hands in hers. "I don't think so, Mutzi. Remember, that happened once before." Marge tilted her head. "You've been thinking about him recently, maybe you...imagined it?"

Mutzi jerked away. "He was in the park, and—he—talked to me."

Marge's eyes widened. "Oh, my goodness. What on earth did you say to him?"

"Nothing. I ran away."

"Oh, Mutzi." Marge pulled her twin into a hug. "You poor thing. I don't know whether to be happy or sad for you."

"That makes two of us."

Chapter Thirteen

ollecting items for the local food bank in Dahlonega had kept Mutzi busy the week since her unexpected visit with Sam. With the last of a dozen bags secured in place, Mutzi closed the trunk and turned to her sister. "You sure you don't want me to come along?"

"No. You've done more than your fair share. Take a break." Marge climbed into the driver's seat. "A few of the gals are meeting me there to help unload. We've got it covered."

"Okay." Mutzi turned toward the front door just as the landline phone rang. She hurried up the steps, reaching it by the fourth ring. Breathless, she mustered, "Hello?"

"Hi. It's me."

The deep, raspy voice made her freeze in place. "Hey." It was all she could mutter in reply. She'd spoken to Sam a few times since their meeting in the gardens. The calls had been brief, awkward exchanges about the weather and who still lived in the area. She'd ended each call pretending to have something urgent to do.

After the third call, Sam had acknowledged her

avoidance and pressed Mutzi to see him. Knowing she couldn't keep shunning him, she'd relented, agreeing to have dinner with him at the historic Smith House Inn tonight.

"What time should I pick you up?"

Mutzi gripped the cordless phone and walked around the room. "I don't know if I can do this."

"Please, Mutzi. Meet with me this once. If you're unhappy with what I tell you, I'll bring you home and I won't bother you again."

Could it be that simple? She knew better. Her love for Sam hadn't faded in half a century, even believing he was dead. Now that she knew he was alive, life would never be the same again.

When she didn't respond, Sam continued. "You do still have feelings for me, don't you? I saw it in your eyes."

Mutzi pressed her lips together, unwilling to lie. "I don't want to be hurt again." She closed her eyes, feeling his blissful kiss on her lips.

"I'll never hurt you again. Please, give me a chance."

She swallowed hard and summoned the courage. "I'll be ready at six."

"Bless you, Mutzi. I'll see you then."

Mutzi continued to circle her room trying to calm her nerves. She stopped abruptly and opened her nightstand drawer. The stack of envelopes that filled the space had yellowed over the years. One by one, she removed each letter and read it, her hand shaking and tears staining the pages as she revisited the intensity of his love for her. What could he possibly tell her? How could she trust that he wouldn't break her heart again?

"I'm back, Sis," Marge called from the foyer.

Mutzi gathered the letters and stuffed them back into the drawer. She stepped into the bathroom and dampened a washcloth, blotting the trail of tears from her blotchy cheeks. By the time her sister came into her room, she'd opened the closet door and was staring at the menagerie of clothes.

Marge stepped closer. "Have you decided what you're wearing tonight?"

Flipping hanger after hanger of mismatched clothes, Mutzi sighed. "I don't know why I ever agreed to meet him." She pulled out her favorite blouse—a tangerine, polka dot pull over—and put it back, pushing it aside and grabbing another, a striped gabardine jumper.

Marge moved next to her and withdrew a silky indigo blue blouse with ruffles down the front and a pair of black pants—the one's she'd insisted Mutzi buy to wear on special occasions. "This blouse always looks good on you. It brings out the sapphire in your eyes. Wear it with your white cardigan and your black flats."

Mutzi held up the combo and nodded approval. "What could he possibly tell me that would explain his disappearance? I don't know if I can forgive him."

Marge placed her hands on Mutzi's shoulders and locked eyes with her. "It will be okay. Just listen to Sam. Your heart will know what to do next."

"I crumble when he talks to me, when he touches my hand. How am I supposed to keep a clear head when I fall apart?"

A touch of a smile spread across Marge's face. "I understand, Mutzi. I felt the same way about George. Sometimes, I'd be so mad at him, I wanted to smack him. All he had to do was say something sweet or wrap his strong arms around me and I melted into one big puddle. That's what love does to us."

Mutzi shook her head and chuckled. "That was really helpful."

Marge grinned, then shrugged her shoulders, dropping them as she sighed. "I remember Sam being a good guy, one of those rare fellows who was always polite and helpful. He treated everyone with respect. You were your happiest when you were with him. I can't believe he ever wanted to hurt you." She tilted her head, her eyes pleading. "Give him a chance to explain."

Mutzi ushered Marge out of her room. "Go on. I need to get dressed."

A half hour later, Mutzi headed to the kitchen where Marge was removing a sheet of cookies. The sweet scent of peanut butter and chocolate tickled her nose.

Her sister turned, gave her quick glance up and down, and then winked. "You look really nice."

Mutzi adjusted the cardigan and glanced at her reflection in the overhead oven. "Not too bad for an old spinster." She jumped when the doorbell rang.

"Looks like your date is here."

"It's not a date." She released a deep sigh. "Wish me luck."

Marge's eyes darted to Mutzi's hands. "You're not wearing the ring, are you?"

"Not a chance."

As Mutzi opened the door, her legs began to tremble. She gripped the handle to steady herself. Despite the years that transpired, she felt an instant reminder of the many times Sam had stood outside her childhood home, waiting for her.

Sam grinned, flashing his tantalizing dimple. "Wow. You take my breath away." His brown sports jacket and dress pants hung on his thin frame. The maroon dress shirt added a hint of rose to his cheeks.

She drew in the enticing scent of his aftershave and closed her eyes briefly.

"Shall we go?" He raised an arm waiting for Mutzi to take hold of it.

"Don't start charming me before you even feed me." She cast him a sideways glance. "Looks like you've missed a meal or two."

Sam didn't respond. They rode in silence for a few blocks. Each time he glanced at her, his blues eyes glistened, reflecting the sun as they drove into it.

"I'm glad you decided to join me tonight. I know it wasn't an easy decision."

Mutzi nodded her head in agreement, afraid to open her mouth for fear of what might come out. Questions, fueled with emotions spun in her head, accelerating her heart rate with each passing mile.

She withdrew a tissue from the small clutch purse Marge loaned her and dabbed at her forehead. "Hey, you're going the wrong way. You needed to turn left at that last light."

Sam glanced at Mutzi. *Damn that dimple.*

"I hope you don't mind. I thought we should find a quieter place to talk." He squeezed the steering wheel. "When I suggested the Smith House, I'd forgotten they serve family style dinners. If I remember right, sometimes they even seat you with other people."

Leave it to Sam to think things through. "Yeah. I

didn't think about that."

He slowed the truck and looked at her again. "I heard the food is good at Montaluce Estates & Winery. We should get there in time to see the sun setting over the vineyards."

Mutzi raised one brow. "Sunsets and vino. You think that's going to sooth my spirit and make me forget that you left me all alone?" She pressed her lips tight to keep from saying more.

The dimple disappeared from his cheek. "I'm sorry. Not a day has gone by..." Sam swallowed hard. "I've loved you every day, whether you knew it or not."

The confession increased the thunder pounding in Mutzi's chest. "But not enough to come back for me?" The words spewed from her mouth before she could stop them.

The years of guilt, thinking she'd caused his death, the excitement of seeing him again, and then the anger of knowing he'd chosen to abandon her scrambled her mind.

"You deserve an explanation. Can we wait until we get there?"

She scratched at the hairline of her neck, even though it didn't itch. "It's been fifty years. What's another 20 minutes?"

Sam squirmed. His knuckles turned white from his grip. He opened his mouth, then closed it. After a long pause, he spoke. "How have you been?"

The question added to Mutzi's irritation. "We've covered that when you called last week." She yanked the snug seatbelt away from her throat. *Why had she agreed to meet with him?* The collar of her blouse felt too tight, as if it were strangling her throat. She gasped for air. "Pull over. Now!"

Sam's head snapped toward Mutzi as the truck jerked toward the soft shoulder. "Are you sick?" He maneuvered back onto the pavement and turned on his blinker. Pulling into a nearby empty lot, he shoved the gear into park.

Mutzi struggled to release the seat belt with both hands. Sam reached across and pressed the clasp, setting her free. She flung the door open and jumped out. With her arms wrapped tight around her body, she paced in circles.

Sam got out and hurried to her side. "Mutzi. What can I do? How can I help?"

It took a few minutes for her to catch her breath. She bent forward and sucked in air, Sam standing inches from her. When her breathing slowed, she extended her arms out to distance him. "We need to do this now. I can't wait until later."

Sam nodded his head. "All right." He glanced toward the road and back. With the passenger door still ajar, he pointed to it. "How about if you sit there and

I'll stand here."

The offer suited Mutzi. She wasn't sure how long she'd remain upright otherwise.

Sam wiped his brow and straightened his jacket. He heaved a sigh and met Mutzi's stare. "I left Vietnam less of a man, not the same young one you knew. I was injured—" Sam ran a hand through his hair. "Severely." His chest rose and fell, releasing a deep breath. "I had nothing to offer you by coming back."

A parched lump formed in Mutzi's throat. "That wasn't for you to decide. If you had told me—"

"You would have insisted on waiting for me." Sam reached into the back of the pickup and grabbed a bottle of water, handing it to Mutzi. "I was crippled. Damaged goods. I was angry and didn't want pity, from anyone." His head dropped low and he closed his eyes. "I lost my leg. As hard as that was to accept, it was nothing compared to..." Lifting his head, he continued. "I lost my ability to give you what you...what *we* wanted most in life."

Mutzi contemplated his declaration in silence. They'd planned out their lives together. He'd help his dad on the farm and save his money to buy a home in the country with a big porch and five acres on which to raise their six children. Six chil—the realization stabbed her like a knife.

He glanced at her, a tear trickling down his cheek. "A sterile cripple who couldn't give you babies."

Mutzi gasped and cupped her hands over her mouth, involuntarily glancing toward his legs, unable to speak.

Sam stepped closer. "Everything we dreamed, disappeared in the jungle that night. I didn't want to live. I couldn't face you, or my parents. I'd failed everyone and I couldn't live with the thought of ruining your life or being a burden to them." He shook his head at the recollection. "The news of my parents' deaths from the car accident devastated me even more."

The words tore at her heart as she choked back tears. How cruel life had been, to both of them. She clutched at her stomach as if a dagger stabbed her hollow womb. For years, she'd considered his sudden disappearance another punishment for taking the ring. Her letters, returned as undeliverable, reinforced her beliefs. Would it have been any better had she known? What would she have done if he'd told her? He was right. She would have stayed by his side, no matter the cost.

She looked away, gazing at the dusty hillsides as scenes from her life flickered past. Unable to deal with the painful memories the conversation dredged up, she numbed her mind, pushing the agony back into its long concealed space. She couldn't tell him now. Perhaps another day, another time. Her chin trembled as she regained the courage to speak. "Go on." Her voice quivered. "Finish."

Sam cleared his throat. "I refused a medical discharge. I convinced them to let me stay in the Army. They reassigned me to Korea, as a chaplain. That's where I met Song Lee." He glanced at Mutzi, then back toward the road.

Her body recoiled at the disclosure. She took a drink, replaced the cap, and squeezed the plastic bottle, closing her eyes briefly. Of course he'd married. She'd tried to prepare herself, but it hurt more than she'd anticipated. She nodded her head for him to continue.

"She'd been physically and sexually abused by an American soldier. He'd tortured her and left her for dead, on the ground...like a trampled rose." Sam sucked in air, his body shaking as he continued. "My heart broke watching her suffer, shunned by her own people, and frowned upon—damaged goods. I tried to comfort her with my spiritual words. As months passed, her physical wounds healed and I came to know her spirit."

He pressed his lips tight, glancing up to the sky to fight back tears. "I couldn't leave her there knowing she'd be rejected the rest of her life because of what that man did to her. I couldn't."

Mutzi listened without commenting. The deep compassion for the woman touched her heart. What could she say? As much as she wanted to hold on to her anger, his gentle spirit defined him and made her love him more. Two damaged souls finding solace and support in the midst of war. Even *she* felt compassion for the woman.

"I told her about you, how I loved you and only you...forever. Even with our cultural differences, she understood. We were married so she could leave her country. She stood by my side when I was transferred from place to place. Unselfish to a fault, she cared for others and put them first. She never pressed me for more than I could give her."

Mutzi dabbed at her damp cheeks. "Where is she now?"

"She lost her battle with cancer earlier this year." Sam withdrew a handkerchief and turned away as he sobbed.

"I'm sorry, Sam." Mutzi got out of the truck and walked closer to him, touching his back in an effort to comfort him.

His eyes met hers and he nodded toward the sunset. They watched its silent descent beyond the hills. Purple rays danced amidst the scattered clouds.

As darkness settled in, Sam continued to stare at the horizon. "Her dying wish was that I return to

Dahlonega and find you. I never understood it, but she insisted you were still waiting here for me." Sam looked back at Mutzi and the last fifty years melted in his pleading eyes. "Please tell me it's not too late."

Mutzi reached for his hands and squeezed. "I love you Samuel Parks. Always have, always will."

Chapter Fourteen

*T*he Community Center buzzed with hundreds of shoppers looking for holiday bargains. Mutzi busied herself selling Christmas bazaar items, unaware she was being watched by a woman wearing a full length mink coat. But Marge had noticed her the moment she entered the room.

When the commotion slowed, the woman neared the table and cleared her throat. "Looks like the sales are going well."

The familiar voice caught Mutzi's attention. "Hey, Rose Ellen." She reached across the table and poked her older sister's arm. "Glad you made it." She looked around. "Where's April?"

Rose Ellen waved her hand toward the street and shrugged. "She dropped me off and went to find a parking place. I wasn't going to walk four blocks to get here."

The comment disappointed Marge, thinking of the hundreds of times she and Mutzi hiked to and from the town square. She squirmed her way between the tables and gave Rose Ellen a hug. "Good to see you, Sis."

"Good to be back." Rose Ellen chuckled as she removed her coat. "Think I actually missed you two." She handed the large fur to Mutzi. "Here. Don't let this drag the floor."

Mutzi took it and bowed. "Of course, your highness."

Rose Ellen cupped her hand and gave a queen-like wave, giggling and enjoying the banter, seemingly oblivious to the frown on Mutzi's face. Another customer approached and Marge focused her attention on the woman.

In the corner of her eye, she saw April worm her way through the crowd and stand next to her mother. "Whew. I was lucky to find a spot between two pickup trucks."

"Hi, April," the twins said at the same time.

Glancing from one sister to the next, a smirk spread across April's face. "Did she tell you yet?"

Mutzi stood taller, her eyes bright in anticipation. "Tell us what?"

"Mom's staying, at least through New Year's." She paused, raising her brows with a pasted smile. "Isn't that great?"

The twins made eye contact with each other. Concern kept Marge from smiling. Could they tolerate each other for a month? They loved Rose Ellen, but they tended to rub one another wrong after three or four days. She managed to muster a smile. "That's...great."

Rose Ellen looked about the room as she spoke. "Think you can handle it, girls?" As if afraid of hearing their answer, she fidgeted with the silk scarf tied around her neck.

"We'll make it work. Won't we, Mutzi?"

"Sure."

The less than enthusiastic response from her twin added to the tension that seized Marge's neck muscles.

Adjusting the purse hanging from her shoulder, Rose Ellen announced, "I'm going to shop around and look for some tchotchkes—you know—dust collectors I really don't need, but will buy anyway."

"Well, if you're looking to drop some cash, you can start here." Mutzi motioned to the adjoining tables. "The Woman's Club needs the business. And don't be cheap. It's a fundraiser."

Rose Ellen glared at her sister for a moment, then looked down and picked up a set of floral placemats. "Did you make these, Marge?"

Marge beamed. "Yes—I did. Do you like them?" She fanned her hand over a large section of home-made crafts. "I made all of the items in this area."

With a glitter-filled globe ornament in one hand

and a pipe cleaner reindeer in the other, Mutzi announced, "I made these."

The oldest sister gave the items a cursory glance. "You're both so talented. I could never do something so creative."

The statement brought Marge to a halt, amused and surprised that Rose Ellen had any interest in making crafty things. "Really?"

The suggestion brought a different response from Mutzi. "Why would you need to make anything when you can pay someone to do it for you?"

Marge scrunched her mouth, shot a look at her twin, and then turned to Rose. "You've accomplished so much more. You earned an MBA and have your own business."

Rose Ellen shrugged and picked up four of the matching napkins, handing a crisp one hundred dollar bill to Marge. "Getting a degree doesn't come with a special talent."

"Some of us wouldn't know," Mutzi muttered.

Marge studied the large bill, ignoring the snide remark. "I don't have change."

"Just keep it." Rose Ellen's eyes met Mutzi's stare. "Consider it a donation. It is a fundraiser, I'm told."

April stepped in and redirected her mother away from her aunts. "I saw some awesome candles over there. Let's go check them out."

Marge mentally calculated the number of weeks until the first of the year, then shook her head. *Lord, give me strength.*

Customers kept her and Mutzi busy for the next two hours. When the crowd thinned, Marge let out a sigh. "Whew. I'm tired."

Mutzi nodded. "Been a long day, but we sold a lot."

"Just think what we could have done if you had made more of those gold bricks like you did for the Gold Rush Festival. I can't believe so many patrons asked for them. You'll have to do it again next year."

"Maybe." Mutzi bent down and pulled out another box of crafts from under the table, preparing for the round of shoppers on Sunday.

April and her mother appeared within the hour, loaded with numerous purchases. Rose Ellen added her few items on top of her daughter's. "Why don't you take these to your car and pick us up at the door."

"Will do." April juggled the bundles, tucking a bag under her arm and stuffing a few packages into a larger bag.

Mutzi retrieved her coat from the table and handed the mink to Rose Ellen.

Rose Ellen reached for the coat and touched Mutzi's hand. "Thanks, Sis."

The simple gesture pleased Marge. Perhaps the three of them could survive through the extended visit. She rubbed at her aching neck. "I'm getting too old to do this."

"I don't know why you go through all this trouble. Why don't you just ask for donations from some of the wealthy people in town?"

Marge scowled at Rose Ellen. "You just don't get it. This is so much more than a fund raiser. It's a social gathering, a way to stay connected with the community and to meet new people. You can't get that by asking snoot—" Marge caught herself—"people for money."

"Not everything revolves around a big bank account." Mutzi walked toward the exit as April pulled up.

The black sports car gleamed even as the sun faded behind the trees. Mutzi hurried to claim the front seat.

With her hands on her hips and a pout on her face, Rose Ellen turned to Marge. "I guess *we'll* be sitting in back."

Mutzi pulled open the door and hopped in, running her hand over the smooth leather seats. "Does it have road departure mitigation?"

April grinned. "Yep. And a collision mitigation breaking system, too."

"Cool." Mutzi checked all the button and lights on the dashboard as they moved away from the town square and headed up the hill.

Marge looked at Rose Ellen and shrugged. "I have no idea what they're saying."

Mutzi turned and frowned at the two in the back seat, as if they had interrupted her discussion with April. She continued. "How about active park assist?"

April nodded as they rounded the corner and pulled up to the house. "Watch this." With her hands off the steering wheel, the car maneuvered itself into the limited parallel parking spot.

"That's so cool." Mutzi turned toward the back seat. "Did you see that? They use ultrasonics and cameras to enable the advanced technology."

Rose Ellen rolled her eyes. "What the heck are you two talking about? Sounds like a foreign language."

Laughter rose from April and Mutzi as they got out of the car.

"It's the twentieth century, gals. Get with it." Mutzi walked around the car and admired it. "It's a beauty."

"Thanks." April popped the trunk and pulled out three large suitcases.

Rose Ellen wiggled out from the back seat and stood next to her luggage. "Could you take one of those, Mutzi? I don't want to throw my back out."

Mutzi picked up one of the bags. "But you don't care if I do."

Marge pulled her shoulders tight and relaxed them

in an effort to release some stress. *How on earth are we going to manage a month-long visit?*

Once inside the house, Marge hung up her coat and hurried into the kitchen, calling out to the others. "I've got a pot of vegetable beef soup in the slow cooker. We should be ready to eat in about thirty minutes."

When April returned from taking the second over-sized bag to her mom's room, she stopped and poked her head into the kitchen. "You'll only need three place settings." She waved as she rushed out the door.

"Where are you going?" Rose Ellen called out as she walked into the foyer, just as the door slammed. She turned toward the kitchen. "I can't believe she just did that."

Marge shrugged. "Maybe she's going to meet Paul. Sure hope they get back together."

Rose grunted. "She's better off without him." She gazed out the front door. "It would be a shame to cancel the wedding, though. I was so looking forward to a big gathering with lots of fancy decorations."

The buzzer went off, signaling the oven had reached the appropriate temperature. Marge shoved her hands into an oven mitt and picked up the loaf pan, placing it on the center rack. "Now, Rose Ellen. You know April doesn't want all that fancy snazzy stuff. If they do get back together, don't push her on that, please?"

The warning fell on deaf ears as Rose Ellen turned and walked away. "I'm going to my room to freshen up. Call me when dinner's ready."

"Hmpf." The noise escaped Marge's lips as she removed the oven gloves and walked to the dining room. *She could have at least offered to set the table. No, not Ms. High Society.*

Mutzi walked in just as Rose Ellen left. She seemed to sense Marge's irritation. "Let me finish that. Go sit down and rest for a few minutes. You've been on your feet all day."

Marge looked up at her sister and smiled. "My *thoughtful* sister. You've been on your feet right beside me. Let's finish it up together and then sit down with a little glass of wine."

"Sounds like a plan."

The twins busied themselves setting the table. Marge opened a bottle of chardonnay and poured two glasses. They relaxed in front of the fireplace, enjoying a few moments of quiet.

Rose Ellen reappeared, standing with her hands on her hips. "Nice of you to invite me to join you." She cocked her head and wrinkled her nose. "Were you at least going to let me know when it was time to eat?"

Mutzi frowned. "Don't get your feathers in a ruffle. We're tired and decided to sit for a few minutes."

Marge stood and walked into the kitchen without responding. She dished up bowls of soup and sliced the artesian bread, layering it on a serving plate. After putting everything on a tray, she carried it into the dining room. The muted tension echoed off the walls, but no one dared speak.

When dinner was finished, Marge walked into the kitchen and gathered the pumpkin Bundt cake and a can of whipped cream.

Mutzi rose and picked up the tray, gathering the bowls and plates, breaking the uneasy reticence. "The soup was delicious, as always, Sis."

"Yes. It was." Rose Ellen placed her napkin on the table and turned to Mutzi. "April said you had something to tell me."

Mutzi nearly dropped the tray. "April's got a big mouth. Not now."

Rose Ellen straightened her back and picked up her napkin. "What is it? Tell me now. I can't stand the suspense."

Marge let out a sigh and sat down. "We're all too tired to have the discussion tonight. It can wait until tomorrow." The statement was useless. She knew her older sister wouldn't relent.

"I won't be able to sleep all night."

Marge watched Mutzi shove the dishes into the dishwasher and slam the door with a thud. When she returned to the dining room, Mutzi pulled out her chair and plopped down.

"It's a stupid thing I did...as a teenager. Can't this wait until tomorrow?"

Marge tilted her head as she looked at Mutzi. "The sooner you talk about it, the better."

Rose Ellen threw her napkin down. "For Heaven's sake. Just be out with it. I can't imagine something you did more than 50 years ago can be that upsetting."

Mutzi nibbled at her dessert, procrastinating. After she swallowed a bite, she jumped up, and excused herself. "I'll be right back."

Rose Ellen slapped a hand on the table. "What's this all about?"

Marge raised her brows and stuffed another bite of cake in her mouth, refusing to answer.

When Mutzi returned, she held a small box in her hand. "Remember the Gold Rush Festival, the one right before Daddy passed? He brought us each a gift?"

"That's so long ago." Rose Ellen frowned. "He bought us lots of gifts."

"Well, he got this one for you, but I switched and gave you mine—little gold studs. This really belongs to you." Mutzi pushed the small box toward her sister and waited.

Rose Ellen opened the box and let out a yelp. "Oh,

my goodness. Daddy got this for me?" Her eyes bulged wide. "It's the ring from the Dahlonega Gold Museum."

Mutzi and Marge's mouths dropped open. "Are you sure?

"When Daddy volunteered at the museum, I would visit with him and stare at it through one of the glass cases. I loved it and begged him to buy it for me. He'd explain that it wasn't for sale, that it was a piece of history. But I didn't care. I begged him for it over and over."

Marge shook her head. "How on earth would he have gotten it?"

Rose Ellen took it out of the box and examined it. "Maybe he stole it. I think I asked him to." The moment the words were spoken, she clasped a hand over her mouth, and met her sisters' stares. "Don't look at me like that. I was young...and spoiled."

Marge dropped her fork. "Our father would never do that!"

Rose Ellen put the ring on her finger, shrugging her shoulders and smiling. "I can't believe he got this for me." She stood and danced around the room, letting the light bounce off the gold piece, twirling around, like a little girl with a new dress.

Irritated, Marge pushed her chair back to get up, and the two collided sending Rose Ellen into the china cabinet. The hutch tipped over and crashed to the floor, nearly taking Marge with it.

Rose Ellen tried to stifle a laugh. "I'm sorry. Are you okay?"

"You think that's funny?" Mutzi's hurried to help Marge. They locked eyes and Marge knew what Mutzi would say before it left her mouth.

"I told you, Sis." Mutzi scowled. "I told you."

Rose Ellen's face scrunched to a frown. "Told you what?"

With her lips pressed tight, Marge lowered her head and tried to dispel the doubt creeping into her mind. *How could so many bad things happen?* She couldn't dismiss the coincidence of Rose Ellen wearing the ring and the hutch falling. She cleared her throat and looked at her older sister. "Mutzi thinks the ring brings bad luck."

"Hogwash. I wasn't paying attention to what I was doing and then you—"

Marge folded her arms tight, feeling the anger rise from her chest. "Don't blame me because you were acting childish."

The twins lifted the hutch to an upright position and inspected it. A chip of wood had broken off, and the beveled glass from one door lay shattered on the oak floor, but otherwise it withstood the fall. They wiggled it into a corner of the room.

Marge stomped into the kitchen and returned with a broom and dust pan. She thrust them at Rose Ellen and glowered. "Make yourself useful."

Rose Ellen raised her brows and pursed her lips. "Sorry. I was distracted by Daddy's generous gift—to me." She grabbed the broom and swept the glass into a pile.

A sneer spread across Mutzi's face as she took the dust pan from Marge to help.

By some miracle, no one was injured. A few of the plates and bowls remained intact, along with some wine goblets. When the last of the mess was cleaned up, they all retired to the living room with cups of coffee.

Rose Ellen slipped the ring off her finger and placed it back in the velvet jewelry box. She set the box on a corner table and folded her hands in her lap. "Tell me more about this superstition of yours regarding the ring."

Mutzi cleared her throat and began. "Every time someone wears it, something bad happens."

Marge watched Rose Ellen purse her lips and shake her head.

Mutzi continued, "Before you dismiss my belief, listen to how many things have gone wrong, starting with the china cabinet."

Rose Ellen listened as Mutzi ran through the many

examples, first telling her own story and then adding the things that happened to Marge and April. She paused, then swallowed hard. "The reverend suggested I give it back to its rightful owner." She lowered her eyes. "I guess that didn't work."

"Maybe I'm not its rightful owner." Rose Ellen opened the box again and looked at the unique ring. "I have to know how Daddy got this. I'm going to the museum tomorrow. Someone must know the answer."

"Victoria Bridges might. She remembers everything."

Rose Ellen appeared to ignore Mutzi's suggestion. "Daddy did love me. He'd do just about anything I asked him. What if it was stolen?" Rose Ellen's eyes grew wide. "How would we ever show our faces in this town again?"

Marge put down her coffee cup with a little more force than she'd intended, splashing liquid onto the table. "Our father did not steal that ring." She dabbed at the spilled liquid with her napkin. "For goodness sake, don't even suggest that around this town. Gossip spreads like wildfire."

With her cup and saucer in hand, Mutzi stood, ready to walk to the kitchen. "All I know is that we'd all be better off without it. You're welcome to take it with you when you go back home, but it's not staying here."

Chapter Fifteen

When the Dahlonega Gold Museum opened at 9:00 a.m., Rose Ellen walked through the doors, browsing around as if she were just another visitor to town. It had changed a great deal since her father volunteered there in the late sixties.

A wall of coins filled the space where the display cases had once been.

"My, this looks nothing like I remember," Rose Ellen noted to the woman dusting the plaques on the wall.

The elderly lady studied Rose Ellen's face. "You're one of the McGilvray girls. Haven't seen you since your pappy died."

"Yes. I'm Rose Ellen. I moved to New York many years ago."

"The museum was sold to the state of Georgia in nineteen sixty-six. Your father volunteered here until he passed in sixty-nine. Yes, they have renovated numerous times since then. Would you like to take a tour? Certainly worth the six dollars."

"I'm afraid I don't have time today. Perhaps another time." Rose Ellen glanced around at the historic markers. "I seem to remember they had display cases with old jewelry and gold pieces."

"Was there something in particular you were looking for? Maybe it's in one of displays on the tour. You really should take it. It's amazing."

"Well, there was this one ring that I was particularly fond of. It had the most interesting little man, panning for gold."

"I don't believe we have that any more. I pretty much know every piece of gold in this place. The state acquired many things during the transition. Perhaps it changed hands at that time."

Changed hands. Little does she know she might be right. "Most interesting." Rose Ellen turned and walked toward the door. "Perhaps I'll come back when I have a little more time."

"How long will you be staying in Dahlonega?"

"At least until the first of the year." She opened the door to leave. "Have a wonderful Christmas."

"You, too. Try to come back for the tour."

She nodded, then let out a groan when she got outside. That had been a waste of her time. *How am I going to find out if Daddy stole this ring?* She'd have to do some more research. It was too important to let it go.

On the way back to Marge's house, Rose Ellen decided to stop at Magical Threads, a yarn and material store. She'd been inspired by her sisters to start a project. Perhaps she'd make stockings for all of them to hang by the fireplace. Surely, Marge would let her use her sewing machine. The bell on the door jingled as she entered.

A plump woman wearing a bright yellow gingham apron greeted her. "Good morning."

"What a busy little store." Rose Ellen swept the crowded room with her eyes and smiled. "So many things for such a small place."

"I've never seen a bolt of material I didn't love, nor a skein of thread I didn't need."

"I see." Rose Ellen eyed a cluttered aisle. "Perhaps you can tell me where I can find quilted Christmas stockings, the kind you cut out and sew together."

The woman pointed to the right. "There's a large selection in the corner by the quilting fabrics. Do you want me to come help you find them?"

"No. That's okay. I'll browse through them and let you know if I need you to cut something."

Rose Ellen wiggled her way through narrow, congested aisles of fabrics, finally arriving at her destination. Buried under table runners and tree skirts, some blue material caught her eye. She tugged and pushed, exposing enough of the design to see a pristine white, snow-covered church with a lovely star shining above it. *This is perfect.*

"Yoo-hoo." She waved to the worker who was now at the cutting table. "Would you dig this one out for me?"

The woman wore a broad smile as she made her way to Rose Ellen. "That's one of my favorites." She chuckled. "Of course, they all are."

"I need enough for four."

The merchant hummed as she spread out the bolt and smoothed the edges, lining up the material for a perfect cut. She folded the mound of cloth into a neat pile. "Do you need thread to match? Of course you will."

Before Rose Ellen could respond, the busy clerk hurried down another aisle and grabbed two spools, waved them in the air and pointed to the checkout counter. "I'll meet you over there."

Rose Ellen wove her way around the disorderly piles to the front of the store. She propped her over-sized purse up on the counter and opened it. As if it were a projectile, the ring box flew out, across the counter and onto the floor by the merchant's feet. The woman picked it up and handed it back to Rose Ellen, who opened the box and slipped the ring on her finger, admiring it with a smile.

The woman's brows raised as she eyed the piece of jewelry. "Quite unusual."

"My daddy got it for me many years ago." Rose Ellen reached into her purse again searching for her wallet. When she didn't see it, she stretched the purse open wider and dug through each compartment, frustration growing by the minute.

"This is crazy. My wallet's missing." She looked back to the area where she'd been searching for the stockings. "What could have happened to it?"

"Oh, my. Maybe you left it at home. Do you live far from here?"

"I'm staying with my sisters, Marge and Mutzi. I'm sure you know them. They're always sewing something."

"Oh, yes, of course. Sweet women, your sisters. Why, they've been coming here for years. And if I remember right, your name is Rose Ellen." The woman's face grew serious. "Your father worked at the museum, didn't he?"

"Yes. He volunteered there." An unexpected headache crept up the back of Rose Ellen's head. "I'll have to leave this purchase and come back when I find my wallet."

"Don't be silly. Take it with you and pay me later." She printed out two receipts and handed them to Rose Ellen. "Just write your name on this so I won't forget whose it is and keep the other one so you'll know how much you owe me."

"This is embarrassing. It's never happened to me." Rose Ellen took a pen from her purse and wrote her name and phone number on the paper, handing it to the store owner.

The woman's once-friendly face grew solemn. She reached for Rose Ellen's hand and stared at the ring. Taking in a quick breath and then letting it seep out, she said, "Quite rare, quite rare."

Rose Ellen pulled her hand back. "Yes, it is." The tone of the woman's voice grated on her. "Thank you, I'll be back." Rose Ellen hurried out of the store.

All the way back to Marge's house, Rose Ellen replayed the look on the woman's face when she saw the ring. She recognized it. *I know she did. What if Daddy did steal it for me? Now that lady knows who has it. If word gets out, I'll never be able to face anyone in Dahlonega again. I have to find out how he got it.*

Rose Ellen made it back to the house and stood in the foyer, breathing a sigh as she removed her scarf and coat. Marge's voice trailed from the study. Rose Ellen called out, "I'm back."

The chatter stopped and Marge appeared. "You've been shopping. Buy something good?"

Rose Ellen clutched the bag close to her chest. "It's a surprise. I was hoping you'd let me use the sewing machine later."

Marge stifled a chuckle. "*You're* going to sew?"

Rose Ellen whipped her hand to her hip. "I took Home Economics in high school."

"I'm sorry. I forgot. Of course you can use it. If you need help, let me know."

Baffled by the conversation she heard when she arrived, Rose Ellen asked, "Is Mutzi here?"

"No. She's taking care of some Christmas business."

"Who were you talking to when I came in?"

"George."

Rose Ellen decided not to pursue the subject. She rushed off to her room. A search of her coat pockets, under the bed and her suitcases revealed no wallet. Nothing. She wandered into the kitchen where Marge layered lasagna noodles in a pan.

"I'm afraid I have a big problem. Actually, maybe more than one."

Marge paused midair with a ladle of sauce. "What kind of problem...problems?"

"The yarn shop lady." Rose Ellen nibbled her bottom lip.

"What about her?"

"She saw the ring. I swear she knows where it came from." Rose Ellen held her breath as if saying more would make her fear come true.

"For goodness sakes. Don't be silly." Marge sprinkled some parmesan cheese as she shook her head.

"But what if she did recognize it? What if someone once suspected Daddy of stealing it?"

"All this energy being wasted on such silliness. Put the darn thing away and be done with it. I'm tired of hearing about it."

Rose Ellen glared at her sister. "You wouldn't say that if you knew what happened today."

Marge washed off her hands and closed her eyes. "Pray tell." She sighed. "What happened now?"

"I went to pay for...for the surprise I bought and when I opened my purse, there was the ring. It flew out." Rose Ellen saw the doubt on her sister's face. "Honestly. It just flew out of it. Then I slipped it on my finger and when I reached in my purse, my wallet was missing. Can you imagine? I've never lost a wallet in my whole life. Why now?" Rose Ellen placed a hand across her chest. "I was mortified. I didn't have any money to pay the poor woman."

Marge set the timer on the stove. "So that's why you went running off to your room when you came in? To look for it?"

"Yes. But it's not there. I looked everywhere. It's simply not here."

"You better start calling the credit card companies."

"I will." Rose Ellen moved her hand to her forehead. "What am I going to do? No cash, no credit cards, no driver's license. Oh, that's the other problem. I have to pay the yarn lady."

"I'll lend you some money until new cards are issued. Your driver's license, now that's a different story. I don't know what you'll use for identification to get a new one." Marge opened the fridge and took out some lettuce. "Fortunately, I've never lost mine either."

Without another word, Rose Ellen rushed out of the room. A few minutes later she returned waving a small blue book. "I've got this. I think they'll accept it at the license bureau."

Marge washed off her hands and dried them. She studied the official document. "When did you get a passport?"

"Right before I left New York to come here. Maybe someday I'll get to use it. I better put it back so I don't lose it, too." As Rose Ellen left the room again, she heard her sister muttering. She stopped to listen, thinking she was talking to her.

"If one more thing happens with that darn ring...oh, goodness, George, listen to me. Mutzi's almost got me believing in her craziness."

Rose Ellen hesitated, then slipped the ring off her finger, tucked it back into the box, and stuffed it into the dresser drawer with her passport. *Just in case.*

Chapter Sixteen

*A*pril pulled her car into the Scott's Downtown restaurant parking lot in Gainesville. She checked her hair in the mirror and applied a fresh coat of lip gloss. The two weeks since she'd hung up on Paul, refusing to let him speak to her, were torture. She missed him. Everything about him. The way he snuggled next to her in bed. The early morning kisses. The enticing scent of his light musk aftershave. Especially how when he smiled, his seductive brown eyes smiled too. She'd finally given in and agreed to meet him for dinner in Gainesville.

Paul's maroon SUV backed into the empty space next to April. She watched as Paul unhooked his seatbelt and climbed out. The tug of war between her gut and her heart kept her frozen behind the wheel. Paul approached her car, his hand lingering on the handle of the driver's door. April looked straight ahead, knowing she'd cave the moment she met his eyes.

"Is it all right if I open your door?" His voice was muffled as he spoke through the closed window.

She swallowed hard, pulse pounding in her temples. Why had she agreed to meet? Was she so pathetic she couldn't make it on her own? She glanced up at him, quick to look away. Shaking her head, she questioned her decision again. Gripping the steering wheel, she yelled aloud. "Why am I here?" Such a stupid question. She knew why. Still, the vulnerability frustrated her.

Why couldn't she be independent like her mother? All the years since the divorce, she'd avoided men and survived just fine. But, April wasn't her mother, she needed Paul. Couldn't imagine her life without him.

When she didn't object further, Paul pulled open the door. "We're here because you still love me, and I love you." He leaned in close enough to brush her lips, and then backed away. "Sorry. I've tried to tell them no, but they have a mind of their own." A devilish grin formed on his face.

He knew how to make her laugh. It made it impossible to be serious. She sucked on the inside of her cheeks, trying to mask the smile that wanted to erupt into laughter. "You hurt me. You really hurt me."

"I'm sorry. But if you'll let me explain, I can put an end to that hurt. I promise."

April moved a leg to get out and Paul offered his hand. She refused it and stepped out. He remained close enough for her to feel his breath on her neck and she shivered in response.

"I've missed you, April." His piercing eyes tore through her defenses.

Her unshed tears stung and the lump in her throat blocked her response.

Paul reached out and took her hands in his, the smile fading as he spoke. "Do you want to talk now?"

The warmth of his touch rippled through her body. April swallowed hard and paused. She wasn't ready to be disappointed with his excuse, not yet. What if it was the last time they spoke? She wanted more—more time with him—before ending it. "I think I need a drink first."

Paul gave her hands a squeeze. "Thank you for agreeing to see me."

"I hope I don't regret it."

"You won't. I promise."

Paul wrapped an arm around April's shoulder. There was no use pretending. She could no more leave this man than cut off her arm. She closed her eyes for a moment, wanting to enjoy the comforting security of his closeness. Pride made her jerk away from his embrace. "No."

Paul's head dropped with the sudden rejection. He nodded and moved a step away, giving April a little distance as they walked to the restaurant's entrance.

Once inside, the maître d' greeted Paul. "I have your table as requested."

He showed them to a remote table near a window, overlooking a garden of spectacular Japanese maples.

"I called ahead and asked for some privacy."

The thoughtful gesture was another of Paul's extraordinary traits she'd miss. Always planning ahead to make each outing special. So considerate of others and their needs. *How can this be the same man who broke my heart?* April studied his face, trying to imagine how she could forgive him. The other, often stronger voice fought back. *How can I not?*

Once the waiter took their order, Paul tilted his head and looked at April. "Are you still in pain from the accident?" He fumbled with his napkin. "I've been so worried about you."

"My ribs still ache." She tucked a strand of hair behind her ear. "Some wounds take a long time to heal."

Paul reached across the table, gently touching April's hand. "I'm sorry. I still don't know how it happened."

His thumb stroked her skin, sending tingles up her arm and she pulled her hand onto her lap. "It what? My accident? Or your affair?"

"April, I—"

"Of course you're going to tell me there was no affair." She turned her head and stared out the window.

Paul held his breath, releasing it slowly. "There was no affair, April." He waited until she looked back at him before continuing. "How did the accident happen?"

"It was stupid. When the news station showed the two of you, I got pissed and took off in the car. Those winding roads don't allow much time to brake when a deer comes charging out of the woods, especially if you're speeding."

Paul shut his eyes and cringed. When he opened them again, his eyes were moist. "The thought of losing you." His voice cracked as he spoke. "You—are my life, April. The most important person."

April straightened her back. His tender reaction almost broke through her defenses, but her unresolved anger persisted. "Then how could you cheat on me?"

The accusation made Paul flinch and his face firmed. "I did not cheat on you. I would never cheat on you. It hurts me that you believe I did."

"How can I believe anything else? I saw you with my own eyes."

Paul pressed his lips together. "Please, just listen."

April saw the pain etched in his face and quietened. "All right, explain it to me, now."

"I'd left my brother's place in Canton at one o'clock, heading straight to your aunt's house. I wanted to surprise you by coming early. About a half-hour later, Josh called saying his car had broken down on his way to meet Priscilla."

Paul paused when the server brought their salads and waited for him to leave. "All morning he'd acted so strange. Nervous, jittery. Couldn't sit still and he kept checking his watch. He wouldn't tell me what was going on. When he called, he was freaking out, begging me to help him. I couldn't leave him stranded. So I turned around and headed back. I sent you a text saying I'd join you for dessert."

April stabbed at the croutons in her Caesar salad as she listened. "I got that one. Go on."

Paul hadn't touched his food, but he picked up his glass of pinot noir and sipped. "When I pulled up to Josh's car, he rushed up and grabbed the passenger door handle and jumped in shouting, "We have to go back to the house so I can change. I got grease on my suit." His eyes bulged and sweat poured down his neck. I thought he was having a heart attack. I asked him what the heck was going on and he finally spilled the news. He was meeting Priscilla for dinner, in downtown Atlanta, and had made all these special arrangements with the restaurant. My little brother was proposing. He didn't tell either of us because he was afraid we'd let it slip before the event."

The explanation swirled around in April's head. "So you went to dinner with them?"

"Not exactly. He was worried she might say no. I had my doubts, too. Josh would have been devastated, and I wanted to be there for him."

"But, she loves him. Why would she say no?"

"Aw, come on. Priscilla's an amazing woman. A professional. She has her act together, like you. And then there's Josh. The guy who dances like a doofus, wears plaids with stripes, and who still finds putting two sentences together a challenge. He's got a big heart, but—well, let's just say he wasn't overly confident."

"But he's matured a lot in the last year."

"You're right. He has, and sometimes I forget to give him credit for what he's accomplished. Buying a house and holding a steady job are strong attributes." He picked up his wine glass and drained it. "So, I told him I'd wait in the parking lot while they had dinner. He had the ring delivered with dessert."

She tried to picture the scene. "Wait, so you didn't even get to eat dinner on Thanksgiving?"

"No. But Josh came out and got me after she said yes and I went in to congratulate her. I tried to call you, but couldn't get a connection. I found out later there was an outage with the service provider." Paul took a sip of water. "An overload of calls on Thanksgiving, I guess."

April's hand flew to her mouth. His explanation rattled in her brain. Her best friend got engaged and she'd allowed her pride to ruin it. Besides, she'd caused unnecessary anguish for herself and the man she loved.

"I don't know what to say." She stared at him wanting to erase the past few weeks. "You are such a wonderful brother. Not many guys would have done that." She squeezed his hand. "How could I have doubted you?"

Paul twisted his mouth and raised his brows, making a silly face. "I don't know? How could you?"

Remembering the television scene, April's eyes narrowed. "But where was Josh when I saw you two on the news?"

Paul shrugged his shoulders and shook his head. "That must have been when he was taking care of the tab. I walked out with Priscilla and I guess I had my arm around her shoulder. I was so happy for them."

"I can't believe Priscilla didn't tell me."

"She tried, but you blocked her."

April covered her eyes, realizing she'd cut off communication from her best friend for no good reason. "Crap. I've got some serious apologizing to do."

"She'll understand and I know she'll be glad to hear from me. She's been anxious to tell you all the details."

April leaned in, holding his warm cheeks in her hands. "I'm so sorry. I really am. Will you forgive me?"

Paul's lips met hers and the weeks of heartache dissolved like fog dissipating with a sun rise.

Chapter Seventeen

*T*he early morning sun greeted Rose Ellen as she dressed in anticipation of the long day ahead. She removed the ring box from the drawer in her room and considered wearing the ring. The knot forming in her stomach made her tuck it into her purse. With the directions to the Georgia Capitol Museum in one hand and Marge's car keys in the other, she headed out the door, determined to track down more information about the ring without stirring suspicions in Dahlonega.

She'd spent the previous day making a series of phone calls to curators in Georgia. It took a number of unsuccessful attempts before a man, with a strong Italian accent, agreed to meet with her. She hoped he'd be able to discreetly provide her answers to the unsolved mystery of how her father got the ring.

Rose Ellen arrived at the museum before noon. She hurried into the ladies' room to make sure she was presentable. The navy business suit fit snug enough to reveal her curves, something she worked hard to maintain all her life. She removed a piece of lint from her lapel and secured an errant auburn curl before exiting the room.

Rose Ellen hovered in the doorway as Roberto Montelini sat with his back toward the door. His sharply cut salt and pepper hair laid just above the crisp blue collar of his dress shirt. When she knocked, the man stood and faced her. As he stepped away from the desk, Rose Ellen allowed a hint of a smile to form. The handsome gent reached for her hand and raised it to his lips. Rose Ellen felt the temperature of the room warm with his touch.

With one raised brow, he tipped his head. "Belissima signora, it is an honor to meet you, Ms. Preston."

The pleasant Italian greeting caught Rose Ellen by surprise. Finding herself short of breath, she withdrew her hand and let it idle near the neckline of her blouse, feeling her pulse beating faster than normal. "Thank you for agreeing to see me." She glanced around the small office, breaking the spell of his enticing mariner-blue eyes. Numerous plaques on the wall contained impressive credentials awarded to the curator.

"To what do I owe the honor of your visit?" His smooth tone was nearly lyrical.

Rose Ellen narrowed her eyes. Was this silver fox trying to seduce her? She had to admit, it was working. Opening her purse, she withdrew the jewelry box, handing it to Mr. Montelini. "I'm trying to research this antique ring. I think it may have historical value.

"Hmm. Quite unusual." He opened his desk drawer and took out a loupe and studied the inside of the ring. "And what makes you believe this is a historical item?"

"It may have been displayed in a showcase in the Dahlonega Gold Museum." Rose Ellen tried to read his expression, but flecks of teal twinkled from his eyes, distracting her. She chastised herself in silence.

The curator walked toward the window and held the ring above his head. Sunlight danced on his ravishingly thick hair, a trait few men in her age bracket still possessed. *Oh, how I'd love to run my fingers through those tantalizing waves.* She drew a deep breath and looked away to break the spell he seemed to cast over her.

"Much research will be required to provide answers to your questions, Mrs. Preston."

That was smooth. Rose Ellen contained a smile that ached to escape. "*Miss* Preston." Their eyes met and the man offered a slight nod in acknowledgement.

"I'll remember that." He held up the ring and continued, "I will need time to verify its authenticity."

"Of course. I'll leave it with you." Rose Ellen hesitated. *What if Mutzi's fears are right? Should I warn him?* She dismissed the concern knowing he wouldn't be wearing the thing. "I'll be in Georgia for another few weeks." She paused, trying to find the right way to say what was on her mind. "I prefer to keep this between the two of us. Can your research be done discreetly?"

The request seemed to tickle the curator and he chuckled.

"Of course. Your name will not be mentioned, *Miss* Preston."

She extended her hand to say goodbye. "You may call me Rose Ellen."

"Only if you call me Roberto." Once again he drew her hand to his lips and held it there, closing his eyes. "She walks in beauty, like the night, of cloudless climes and starry skies; And all that's best of dark and bright, meet in her aspect and her eyes."

The blood rushed to Rose Ellen's face and she felt it burning her cheeks like a smitten school girl. "Lord Tennyson. Impressive." She fluttered her eyes playfully. "You're quite the charmer." Rose Ellen shifted her purse to the other arm. "Until we meet again."

"I look forward to it. I'll call as soon as I have anything to report."

Rose Ellen nodded and whispered to herself, "Perhaps, even if you don't." She felt the man's eyes follow her as she left and encouraged a slight sway of her hips to entertain him until she reached her car.

It had been many years since a man stirred flutters in her body. She quite enjoyed it. On the drive back to Dahlonega, Rose Ellen turned on some holiday music and sang along to nearly every song, something she hadn't done since moving to New York.

She decided to stop and pay the yarn lady. A few women were gathered at the end of an aisle and hushed when they saw her. Rose Ellen chose to ignore them and instead, focused on a lovely wall tapestry hanging behind the register. A different flower was cross-stitched for each day of the month.

"That is quite beautiful. I can't imagine how much time it took to sew that."

"My momma made that while sitting right here behind the counter. Miss her something terrible." The merchant picked up a stack of receipts and thumbed through them.

"It's Rose."

"Nope. It's Daisy. Today's Thursday." Thelma let out a hearty laugh, loud enough to draw the attention of the group of women. "I'm sorry. I just had the urge to make a funny. Sometimes you have to laugh a little to make it through a day.

Rose Ellen didn't get the humor, but smiled anyway. "It's unfortunate you had to wait for your money."

"Lordy, girl, don't worry about it. People come in here all the time and run a tab." She took the money and tucked it in the cash drawer. "By the way, did you find your wallet?"

"No. As a matter of fact, I didn't." She shook her head, still frustrated with the loss.

"Did you shop somewhere else that day before you came in here?"

Rose Ellen glanced up, a finger resting on her lip as she tried to remember. "It was early and I hadn't—wait, I did go to the Gold Museum first."

The merchant glanced down at Rose Ellen's hand. "Not wearing your ring today." Her voice raised an octave. "The one your *father* gave you. He volunteered there, at the museum, didn't he?"

The question caught Rose Ellen off guard. From the corner of her eye, she noticed the group of woman had moved closer and appeared to be listening for her response. "Not sure why it's of any importance."

Thelma twisted her mouth sideways. "Just being neighborly. If you're done, I need to help someone at the cutting table."

Rose Ellen glanced back at the women, who stared in her direction, and then picked up her purse. "I'm finished. Thank you." The bell on the door jingled as she left. She got into her car and headed to the museum, her mind still replaying the conversation with Thelma.

The Gold Museum stirred with visitors as she entered it. Rose Ellen approached a woman wearing a badge. "Would you please check and see if someone turned in a wallet? I was here the other day and I've not been able to find it since."

The white-haired woman excused herself, disappeared behind a door and returned after a few minutes. "I'm sorry, but nothing has been turned in."

Rose's shoulders dropped in disappointment. "Thank you for checking."

By the time she got back to her sister's house, frazzled from the unsuccessful mission, she hurried toward her room.

As Rose Ellen scurried past the study, Marge called out, "How did it go?"

Rose Ellen stopped, wanting to acknowledge her sister, but not wanting to delay her much needed nap. "Long and exhausting, but interesting." She yawned. "I'm going to lay down for an hour. I'll fill you in at dinner."

"Sounds good. See you about six-thirty."

After hanging up her business suit, Rose Ellen slipped on a soft, crimson-colored robe and laid down, drifting off to sleep in minutes. In her dream, she and Roberto danced across a ballroom floor on a magnificent cruise ship. The two melted together as one, her feet floating as he held her close, whispering melodic Italian nonsense into her ear. She hoped the dream would never end.

A knock on the door brought Rose Ellen back to the

real world.

"Are you awake? It's almost dinner time," Marge called.

"I am now. Be down in a few." Rose Ellen remained on her back reliving the delightful memory of the man's kiss on her hand. He was quite the opposite of the man she divorced thirty something years ago. Her ex didn't have a romantic bone in his body, at least not toward her. He'd saved that for other women.

She got out of bed and went to the mirror, turning sideways to review her figure. "Maybe there are a few surprises left." She smiled at the thought.

Chapter Eighteen

*M*utzi logged off her laptop and closed the lid, pleased another Christmas project neared completion. Along with it came an unfamiliar confidence about the gifts she'd chosen to give this year.

Her spirits soared in the weeks since Sam returned. Little things didn't irritate her as much as before and she found herself laughing more often. She'd even returned to church, surprised to find Reverend Mitch's sermons uplifting and the congregation warm and friendly. She admitted that the release of guilt played a significant role in her new perception.

The world—no—*her* world had changed. For the first time, she felt purpose, not the simple caring for houseplants or critters, which she still found time to do. It was something much stronger, like the projects she worked on had purpose. Along with a new sense of pride, she felt needed. After years of being alone—and lonely, Sam had come back for her. He needed and wanted her. How long had it been since she felt needed?

No longer the odd-one-out at dinner parties, or the

old maid who was too quirky to find a man who could handle her. The man she loved, had always loved, had returned to fill the crater in her soul.

Mutzi even found herself regretting the limited time she'd spent with Rose Ellen. Normally, she'd found ways to occupy herself in order to keep from having run-ins with her older sister. Often the communication between them was strained, like they came from different planets. Rose Ellen focused on image, what others thought of her, and how she influenced the world around her.

Mutzi knew her axis was off center and she didn't care. People could accept her or leave her alone. Their choice. Still, she loved Rose Ellen and knew her time visiting would soon end and for once, it saddened her. She vowed to try and spend more time with her.

Their limited visiting hadn't been Mutzi's fault alone. Rose Ellen had become enamored with that Italian curator. Mutzi imagined their time together had little to do with researching the ring. Too many giggles, blushing phone calls, and late night dinner dates gave it away. Knowing the man had possession of the cursed ring brought Mutzi comfort.

Christmas was just a few days away. When Mutzi wasn't with Sam, she focused on the final preparation of the gifts for her sisters. Marge practically lived in the kitchen, baking and preparing favorite dishes to please anyone who planned to dine with the family on Christmas.

A renewed energy filled Mutzi's spirit for their tradition of exchanging gifts after returning from church services on Christmas Eve. The trio always gathered around a warm fire with a glass of egg nog, each sharing the blessings bestowed upon them during the year. This time, she'd have something special to share.

Always on a limited budget, Mutzi chose to make her gifts. Often, they ended up in a closet, never to be seen again. But this time, she hoped both sisters would cherish what she'd constructed, making the extra time and effort she'd put into each gift worth it. That seldom happened since her mind didn't work like that of most people.

She felt hopeful the results would be different. Her unspoken fear of this being the last year all three would celebrate together still lingered in the back of her mind. *That damn picture. Maybe if I just destroyed it.* Yet, she'd begun to question the power of the superstitions she carried with her each day.

Mutzi headed to the Dahlonega General Store to find some special stationery. With the weather unusually mild for December, she slipped on a Christmas sweater and red and white stripped leggings. The knee-high boots did little to keep her from looking like a candy cane searching for a tree. That was Mutzi, festive and funny.

Finding a gift for Sam challenged her. He was a minimalist and didn't go in for frilly things for the home. Perhaps his new place needed something to make it more inviting. She hadn't had time to make his gift, since she hadn't even known he was alive, much less returning to Dahlonega, until a few weeks ago. Still, she wanted to surprise him with something memorable.

There was nothing on Mutzi's wish list. Her needs were few and her blessings many. As long as she had a roof over her head, food on the table, and a bed to sleep on, she was good. For many years, Marge had been the one to provide that for her. Next year, who knew what was in store, but Mutzi refused to look too far ahead. Today was what mattered. Today, life was good.

As she passed the leather store, Mutzi nodded to the owner, "Morning, Clyde."

"Mutzi." The man frowned and rubbed his unshaven chin. "Have to admit, you were right about the weather. Don't know how you always know."

"Little bit of luck and a lot of arthritis." Mutzi took a few steps and stopped abruptly, turning back.

The elderly man fussed to himself as he cleaned the windows of his store. "Irritates me to no end to admit it."

She chuckled and pretended not to hear him. "Hey, Clyde, do you still dabble in wood working?"

Clyde whipped his head around at the sound of her voice, his cheeks a bright red. "Thought you—never mind. Still manage to get in a little wood working. What's on your mind?"

Mutzi described the gift she wanted to give to Sam. With a plan set in action, she continued on her way.

"Morning, Ger—" She stopped short seeing the slender red-head. "Monte. Where's Geraldine?"

"She's having that baby. Went into labor last night about midnight."

"I'll have to get by and see her. She's sure going to be surprised when she finds out it's not a boy."

"Now, Mutzi. We won't know for sure until it's delivered."

"Oh, it's a girl. Bet my bottom dollar on it." Mutzi strolled down the aisle and looked for some stationery. "Thought you had some fancy letter-writing paper?"

"Just a minute," the young man called out. "A new shipment came in yesterday." He rushed to the back room and came out with a handful of options.

Mutzi thought for a few minutes, browsing at each design and selecting one. As she paid for her purchase, one of her neighbors walked up to her and paused.

The portly woman shifted from one foot to the other. "I'm not one to gossip, but I thought you should know."

Mutzi caught herself before she burst out laughing at the ridiculous denial. "What is it, Mabel?"

"Well." The woman glanced over her shoulder before continuing. "There's a rumor that your sister was wearing a ring that used to be in the Gold Rush Museum. It disappeared some years ago, you know." She raised a brow as if to suggest that Mutzi knew the rest. "Now, I'm sure there's no connection, but your daddy used to work there and...you know how rumors are."

Mutzi surprised herself by not overreacting to the unspoken accusation. No ranting and raving, no throwing things or insulting the woman. She knew the truth and soon everyone else would too. Instead, she stated unequivocally, "You and your friends are wrong. Stop spreading misinformation." Mutzi grabbed her purchase and marched out without looking back, heading straight to the yarn shop.

Thelma and a few of the women, whom Mutzi imagined were involved in the rumor mill, were gathered around the cutting table. Their lively chatter stopped when Mutzi walked toward them. "You gossiping old biddies need to check your facts before stirring the pot. I want this nonsense stopped immediately. Save yourselves the embarrassment. You'll soon find out my daddy didn't steal any ring."

Thelma's eyes widened. "For goodness sakes, Mutzi. What are you talking about?"

"Don't pretend you don't know, Thelma. My sister saw the way you looked at the ring when she was in here last week." Mutzi smacked her hands down on a stack of material with a thud. "Don't *ever* question my father's integrity. I won't have you demeaning my family based on some unfounded theory."

The women stood in silence as Mutzi stormed out of the building.

Sam appreciated the time spent with Mutzi over the past few weeks, but he was grateful to have a day or two to finish his gifts for the woman with whom he longed to spend the rest of his life. It wouldn't be easy for her to adjust to his neat and tidy lifestyle, but he wanted to make her feel welcomed in what he hoped would be their home.

He'd spent many late nights transforming the sunroom into something called a babe-cave. Taking hints from projects posted on the computer, he'd gathered all the necessary tools and hardware to bring it together. It challenged him to step out of his comfort zone of earth tones and pastels and embrace the colorful options he thought would please the love of his life.

He started by painting the walls turquoise and then bolted multi-colored square crates to the wall to hold Mutzi's large collection of books and crafts. The flamboyant scheme, completely opposite of his taste, fit her colorful character. The glitter-covered switch plates almost sent him over the edge, but he managed to ignore his dislike of anything sparkly in order to incorporate her aberrant tastes. More neutral and fitting to his taste, he hung a white indoor hammock in one corner, and an old roll-top desk occupied another.

Sam couldn't wait to reveal the room to her on Christmas. Yet, he continued to struggle with the nagging fear she'd refuse his offer to make his house her home. *Could she, would she, be willing to change her life for him?*

Chapter Nineteen

*T*raffic came to a dead stop. Frustrated and running late, Rose Ellen pulled out her phone and pressed the number 2 on her speed dial. After a quick ring, Roberto picked up.

"Perhaps I haven't been stood up. Is everything all right, my dear?"

The seductive accent made her giggle. "I'm stuck on the highway. There must be a wreck. I'm afraid I don't know what time I'll arrive. Will you wait for me?" She hoped for a positive reply, but could understand if he needed to leave.

"For you, bel fiore, time has no meaning. The vino will keep me warm until your arrival."

Rose Ellen felt her face flush. "Save some for me."

"Shall I keep you entertained with words by Tennyson?"

The thought settled in her heart and made her beam. "Later, Roberto. The cars are starting to move."

"Ah, such delightful news. I await your presence."

What is it about this man that makes me giddy? For years, she'd avoided men, refusing their advances without hesitation. The scars left by her ex kept a fortress around her soul and discouraged suitors from getting close. Yet, something about Roberto shook those walls she'd built and made them crumble.

With the phone tucked inside her purse, Rose Ellen gripped the wheel and pressed hard on the gas pedal. Her heart fluttered as she replayed the call. She'd grown accustomed to the absence of romance in her life. Roberto stirred feelings long buried under business obligations and meaningless dates. Besides, she hoped to hear news about the ring. She'd had sleepless nights worrying about it since Mutzi told her about the gossip spreading through the town.

Rose Ellen knew her father wouldn't have stolen the ring, but the possibility he could have done something so extreme to please his firstborn, still made her feel special. The next few exits flew by as she reminisced. She could feel her daddy's arms hugging her tight as he spun her around the yard until they both fell to the ground.

Deep in thought, the exit to the restaurant appeared quicker than expected. Flustered, she hit the brakes hard to make the turn. After pulling into the parking lot, she checked her makeup and hair, and then hurried inside.

The hostess escorted Rose Ellen to Roberto's table. He stood and reached for her hand. She lingered for a moment, waiting for him to kiss it, and he didn't disappoint. The alluring Italian leaned in and teased his lips across her cheek light as a butterfly's wing and whispered into her ear. "Be still my heart. My beautiful amore has arrived."

The words warmed her cheeks. "Do you charm every woman this way?"

"You are one of a kind, my dear. I've saved my best for you."

Rose Ellen wanted to believe him, but such a fetching man surely had many women at his side. She resolved to enjoy the moment and not concern herself with the past nor the future.

Roberto pulled out the chair and waited for Rose Ellen to take her seat. "I took the liberty of ordering you a glass of their finest white wine. I hope that wasn't too presumptuous."

Their eyes met and all else faded around her. An overwhelming desire to meet his lips made her shiver. She struggled to catch her breath and looked away. *Don't have a damned heart attack. He's just a man.* She berated herself in silence and reached for the crystal glass, taking a sip. "Perfect." Recovering from her foolishness, she asked, "Have you been busy?"

"Ah, yes. My position is demanding. Tedious work, but most enjoyable." He reached across the table and touched her hand.

Rose Ellen pretended it didn't excite her, but it awakened nerves she'd thought she'd buried deep enough to ignore. "What have you found out about the ring? I'm anxious to know."

He stroked her wrist with his thumb and nodded. "Patience, my dear. One must understand, it takes time to retrace the historic tracks of such a fine piece."

Rose Ellen pulled back and folded her hands on her lap. "I thought you must have learned something by now, since you arranged another meeting." Disappointment tempered her mood.

Roberto bowed his head, and then raised his eyes to meet her stare. "I must admit, my intentions were—selfish. I ached to see you again."

The corner of Rose Ellen's lips turned up. "Aren't you the sly little devil? You could have just told me that."

"But you may have refused and then what would I do?" Laugh lines formed around his deep blue eyes.

"Surely, you've found out something."

"Yes. I've learned that I do not know much about Dahlonega, Georgia." He fumbled with his napkin. "It was the site of the first major gold rush. Benjamin Parks was out hunting for deer when he kicked up some dirt and found gold. Apparently, it didn't take long before word spread and gold diggers came from everywhere."

Unimpressed with the information, Rose Ellen frowned. "Anyone who lives in Dahlonega knows that."

The curator leaned in and raised a brow. "I am not from Dahlonega, much less this country. I'm afraid my skills are better suited for other matters." He sighed. "I wish I could devote my life to fulfilling your every desire, my dear. Unfortunately, my current schedule does not afford me the time to find your answers so quickly." He rearranged his silverware. "Perhaps I am not the right person for the mission."

Rose Ellen exhaled. The admission frustrated her, but the fine-looking man intrigued her and she didn't want their time together to end. "I'm disappointed, but I do understand."

With his palm extended, he waited for Rose Ellen to take it. "I'm sorry. Disappointing you does not come easy. I hoped our journey together was just beginning."

Rose Ellen slipped her hand into his. "It does not have to end."

Roberto leaned in closer. "Does this mean you will see me again?"

She searched his features contemplating a response. "It does."

A smile stretched wide across Roberto's face. "The burden upon my heart was lifted with those precious words." He gazed into her eyes. "There is something about you, Rose Ellen, which pulls me toward you, refusing to let you go."

The confession sent electric shocks through Rose Ellen's body. Dare she let him in? She summoned the courage to share her thoughts. "I've felt the same about you. But I don't even know you. How can that be?"

"I don't know. But I have more life in me today, because we met, than the day I was born. I wake each morning with renewed energy and the hope of seeing you again." With a nod of his head, he continued, "The moment is upon us and we must take hold, lest it slip through our fingers. Please tell me who you are, my dear fiore di rosa."

Rose Ellen leaned back and sighed. "Where shall I start? I was born and raised in Dahlonega. It's quite a lovely town, but I wanted something more. I traveled to New York and earned my degrees. My marriage to a narcissistic businessman failed when I found my husband shacking up with his secretary."

Roberto frowned, shaking his head. "Such a foolish man."

Rose Ellen nodded. "We divorced, leaving me to raise a teenage daughter on my own. It wasn't easy, but I did it and I'm proud. Eventually, I opened my own boutique, which has flourished, though I must admit, I'm tiring of the responsibility."

"I applaud your tenacity. It could not have been easy to accomplish both on your own. You are an amazing woman." He studied Rose Ellen's face. "And you have never married again?"

"No. I refuse to settle. Besides, most men find me intimidating."

"I find you intriguing." Roberto stared into her eyes. "I want to know more. Have you traveled abroad?"

Rose Ellen closed her eyes, visualizing the unfulfilled dreams she held in her heart. She seldom allowed herself to engage in such thoughts, for when she did, disappointment overwhelmed her. *Do I trust this man enough to share my secret desires?* She opened her eyes and searched his face for the answer.

After taking a sip of water, she continued, "I have not traveled abroad. I hunger to visit Italian cafés, sampling delectable olive oils and cheeses, and to sip robust wines while sitting on a Tuscany hillside." Rose Ellen placed a hand on her chest and exhaled, feeling a sense of relief sharing her long preserved thoughts.

The tender gleam in his eyes made her feel as if he journeyed with her. "You seem like a woman who goes after what she wants." He tilted his head, a gentleness settling in his face. "So why haven't you done that?"

Rose Ellen hesitated, deciding whether or not to risk more exposure of her heart. "It would be a waste of money without the romance." She felt a blush rise in her cheeks. "I haven't had any of that for—more years than I care to mention."

Roberto's eyes grew moist. He picked up his half-filled glass of wine and swirled it, his gaze shifting to some faraway point beyond the confines of the room.

She watched him drift way, as if traveling to another place. "What is it, Roberto?"

"My Rose, my dear, sweet bel fiore. It is not possible for this to be real." His penetrating eyes captured hers. "So long I have waited for such a woman. It must be fate that brought our worlds together, for no two people were meant to be joined more than you and I."

A slight gasp escaped her parted lips. She ached for this to be real, but prudence delayed a quick response. This man threatened to break through the shield built around her heart, his roguish smile urging her to believe his sincerity. Pulled into the dance, one foot glued to the floor, she begged for a sign, some reassurance. "Why do you say that? You know so little about me."

"What I know is what my heart speaks to me. You are strong and resilient like the cypress trees that grace the Tuscany hillsides filling your dreams." His voice broke as if it pained him to continue. "When I close my eyes, I dream of taking that same journey with the woman who holds my heart." He drew in a deep breath. "I envision standing in Paris, on a bridge, the Pont des Art Bridge—"

Rose Ellen completed his sentence. "Putting a lock on it, with the one you love." Her heart swelled.

Roberto's eyes glistened as he leaned closer, his face glowing with excitement. "Yes."

"That's always been *my* dream." Rose Ellen's heart raced. The two stared into each other's eyes, and she began to allow herself to hope, even trust his intentions.

Roberto lifted his glass and waited for his dinner mate to follow. "To dreams that were meant to come true, at last."

Chapter Twenty

*A*pril carried her two suitcases to the foyer. Not seeing anyone, she called out, "I'm leaving now." She looked around at the place she'd called home for the past few weeks and sighed. The large Victorian house welcomed anyone who visited. She was no exception.

Marge came in from the study and wrapped an arm around her niece. "I hate to see you go, but I'm so glad you and Paul got back together. I've always liked him."

"Me too. He's the best." April wrapped her aunt in a bear hug. "I'll be back for Christmas. I wouldn't miss it."

"Bring Paul with you."

"Oh, he'll be here. He loves your cooking." She patted her midsection. "I'll need extra time in the gym to lose the five pounds I gained since I got here. But, it's always worth it."

Mutzi made her way into the foyer and patted April's shoulder. "You could afford to put on another five pounds. Skinny as a rail, girl."

Rose Ellen appeared with her hands on her hips. "Don't encourage her to gain weight. She needs to drop a few more."

"You've always been a little crazy and much too bossy." Mutzi ducked as Rose Ellen swatted at her.

April chuckled as she picked up her bags and headed out the door, pausing to give each of them a peck on the cheek.

"Good thing you sisters all get along. Might be some wild cat fights around here if you didn't." She laughed heartily as she went down the stairs. "Take care girls. Love you."

The anticipation of being back with Paul made her tingle all over. She peeked in the mirror, obsessing over her hair and makeup as if it was their first date. When she was a few blocks away from their condo, she called him. "Want to help me drag in some of my stuff? I'll be there in a few minutes."

"Sure. I'll watch for you. I'm ready and waiting," Paul added a sexy growl.

"I can't wait to snuggle with you under a cozy blanket. I've missed that."

"Me too." Paul cleared his throat and after a brief pause, he added, "We've got something to talk about when you get here."

The change in his tone did not go unnoticed. "I hope it's nothing bad." A sense of insecurity still lingered in April even though Priscilla had confirmed what happened Thanksgiving night.

"Actually, I think you'll like it."

She squealed in delight. "I'm coming down the street now. See you in a minute."

Paul was standing by their assigned parking place when April pulled up. He walked around the car and opened her door before she had a chance to exit.

"Always the gentleman. How'd I get so lucky?"

"I'm the one who got the best part of this deal." He pulled her close and kissed her with a passion she'd been missing.

She nestled her head on his chest and drew in the musk of his aftershave. "Hmmm. I've missed that."

"Me, too. We better get out of the street. The neighbors will tell us to get a room."

April grinned. "Not a bad idea."

Paul lifted her suitcases and nudged her toward the front door. "I know just the place."

Much like her mother, curiosity drove April crazy. She stopped abruptly, causing him to stumble to keep from stepping on her. "So what do we need to talk about?"

"Not yet." He nodded for her to move. "Let's get this stuff inside. Don't ruin my surprise."

April grinned with anticipation. She loved Paul's playful romanticism.

The scrumptious smell of rosemary filled her senses as she held open the door so Paul could get through with the luggage. Fine china and red taper candles graced the table, while a soft saxophone melody drifted from the stereo.

April turned to Paul. "Do you know how much I love you?" She wrapped her arms around his neck and smothered him with kisses. "You're spoiling me."

"I wanted to show you know how much I missed you."

"Thank you. I don't deserve it, but thank you." She walked around the table into the kitchen. Roast beef surrounded by candied carrots rested on a platter. She peeked in a pot releasing steam from cooked asparagus. Lifting the lid on another, enticing garlicy aroma tickled her nose as she stuck a finger in and drew out a dab of smashed potatoes. April turned and wrapped her arms around Paul. "All of my favorites. You are something else."

He pulled her closer and whispered, "Wait until you see what I've made for dessert."

She wiggled her brows friskily. "Too bad. I had a special dessert in mind for you."

His grin spread wide. "Mine can wait." Paul pulled out a chair for April and bowed. "For you, my dear." Before he sat down, he popped the cork on a bottle of champagne and filled each of their crystal flutes.

April observed the attention to every detail he'd made in preparing for her return. She vowed to never doubt his love again.

Paul raised his glass. "To second chances and always talking things out."

April tapped his glass. "Always. I promise." She took a sip and asked, "So, what do we need to talk about?"

"I was going to wait until later, but I forgot you have no patience." He laughed. "I've been thinking about the wedding. I've got a suggestion I think you'll like."

"Ooh. Tell me more." April listened as he described his plan in detail. When he finished, she jumped up and danced around the room in celebration. "I love it!"

Chapter Twenty-One

*M*utzi gazed at the embers in the fireplace as they snapped and crackled, flames dancing to the slow music playing in the background. She snuggled close to Sam on the sofa, the two relaxing in quiet thought. She glanced sideways at him. Somehow, the flecks of grey in his hair made him even more attractive. The distance and time away from each other had dissipated like the newspaper Sam had used to start the fire. "This is nice."

The corner of his mouth lifted, revealing a half smile. "We could do this every evening." Sam wrapped an arm around her shoulder.

Mutzi's back stiffened with the suggestion. Anticipating the direction the conversation would take, she leaned forward and heaved a sigh, unsure if she was ready to address the unresolved concerns that stirred in her stomach.

Sam's arm fell behind her. "What is it, Mutzi?"

She got to her feet and wandered closer to the fire, picking up the metal poker and stirring the logs. "There are things I'm still working out in my head."

Sam moved to the edge of the couch. "Can we talk about those things? Maybe together we can resolve them."

She continued to face away from him, focused on stirring the ashes. "I changed when you left. I've got a lot of quirks, things that cause me anxiety, things that will probably drive you crazy the more we're together."

Sam stood and moved toward Mutzi, not crowding her, but making his presence known. "I've always loved your uniqueness. But something's weighing heavy on your mind. We can't work it out until you share it with me."

How could she tell him? She'd run the conversation over and over in her mind and it sounded ridiculous. Yet, it burdened her and kept her from moving forward. "Marge calls them superstitions."

Sam stepped closer and placed his hands on her shoulders. "We give our fears different names. That doesn't make them less important. I won't judge you. But I'd like to know what they are."

She leaned back into the comfort of his warm touch. After a few moments of silence, she continued. "I don't know how much longer I have."

Sam spun Mutzi around, accidentally knocking the poker from her hand. It dropped to the floor with a thud. "Are you ill?"

Immediately, she was sorry she'd been so blunt. Mutzi watched his face flush bright red and his brows draw tight making a vertical crease in his forehead. "No—not that I know of—I *feel* okay." She looked away. "I didn't want to tell you. You just lost your wife."

Sam released the breath he'd held and pulled her close. "What makes you think something is going to happen to you?"

"I received a sign." She looked at his face, awaiting his reaction.

The crease eased. "Was it a premonition?"

She heaved a sigh. "Not exactly. It's hard to explain."

Sam touched her cheek and kissed her forehead. "Do you remember when you started worrying about this?"

The tenderness etched in his face encouraged her to continue. "A couple months ago, I was going through some photos, working on a project for Marge's Christmas present. I found a picture someone took on my camera of me and my two sisters." Mutzi's heart pounded in her chest as she closed her eyes and envisioned the trio.

Sam tilted his head. "What was it about the picture that bothered you?"

Answering the question made her stomach queasy. "I was in the middle."

Sam frowned and ran a hand though his hair. "I'm

not following you. How is that significant?"

Mutzi held a hand on her stomach, trying to contain the ache that grew as she spoke. "It means I'm going to be the first to die."

Sam quieted for a moment, then lifted Mutzi's chin. "I've never heard that one before. Did you read it somewhere?"

"I spend a lot of time on the internet." Her voice quivered as she spoke. "I've never let anyone take a picture of us all together since reading about it, but somebody did." She stared into Sam's eyes. "Do you think it's true?"

He held her face in his hands. "I don't know, but I can tell it's bothering you. And anything I can do to help you work through it, I will."

Her eyes brimmed with tears. "I've been trying to get things in order, just in case. I gave away some of my things." She swiped at a tear trickling down her cheek. "I tried to give away that stupid ring, but it didn't work. I didn't want my sisters to find it after I'm gone, because it brings bad luck."

"I remember you wrote to me about a ring. The one that was meant for Rose Ellen, right?"

"Yes. Ever since I stole it, my life has been a disaster. My dad got sick and died, you disappeared, and..." Mutzi paused, sucking in a deep breath. "Too many things to tell you about, but Marge ended up with it and some crazy things happened to her, too. She gave it to April and she had a bad car accident."

"I can see why you'd think those things are all related. Sometimes, unfortunate things happen to good people." He paused for a moment, then continued. "What if all those bad things that happened were merely part of life's challenges? Part of the journey?" He held her shoulders and peered into her eyes. "Left alone with our fears, they magnify, until they consume us. Is it possible that's what happened to you?"

Mutzi thought about his question. She wished she could believe it was true. Her faith in God had shattered when her father died. Everything seemed to fall apart. She stopped praying, stopped believing anything good could ever happen again. "So, maybe I'm not going to die soon?"

Sam drew her close and tucked a strand of hair behind her ear. "Here's what I do know. We are here today. None of us know when we will be called, but however long we have, I want to spend every minute of it with you."

She heaved a sigh and wrapped her arms around his waist. "So maybe I can eat tomatoes on Tuesday?"

The words made Sam chuckle. "We could test that one out pretty easy." He reached into his pocket and withdrew a handkerchief, dabbing away the remaining tears that dampened her face. "Feeling better?"

With a nod of her head, she stood on her tippy toes and planted a kiss on his lips.

Chapter Twenty-Two

*O*nly one car remained in the parking lot of the church when Mutzi arrived. With everything that had happened since her last meeting with the reverend, she'd decided another visit was in order. "Morning, Rev."

A broad smile spread across the man's face. "It's good to see you again so soon. Please, come in. I was just fixing myself a cup of coffee. Would you like to join me?" He motioned for her to follow him.

Mutzi obliged. "Sounds good." Once in the kitchen, she sat down, watching as he measured the grounds and filled the pot. "Well, I did it. I gave the ring to Rose Ellen."

The reverend glanced over his shoulder at Mutzi. "And how did that go?"

"Not as bad as I thought. You were right. Marge fussed at me a little, but then she forgave me. And Rose Ellen didn't seem the least bit upset. That's a whole different story I'm not going to get into today."

Reverend Mitch handed Mutzi a steamy cup. "Cream or sugar?"

"Naw. Why mess with a good thing." She took a sip and set the cup down. "Guess you heard that Sam

Parks is back in town?"

"Yes, he surprised me with a visit." The reverend settled into a chair and tipped his head, looking at Mutzi. "How are you doing with that?"

Mutzi scrunched her lips and met his eyes. "It's like a miracle. I can't believe he's here, he's alive. It changes everything."

"God works in mysterious ways. And you have no ill feelings toward him for leaving the way he did?"

"Sam's always had a big heart. I can't blame him for what he did." She wrapped her hands around the cup, staring off.

Reverend Mitch rose and went to the counter, returning with a box of donuts. "What will you do now? Do you still care for him?"

Mutzi selected a cinnamon coated cake donut. "I still love him. Always have." She took a bite and chewed, thinking of the real reason she'd come. "He wants us to marry."

"And how do you feel about that?"

She sighed. "I want to be with him. But, I'm not sure he's prepared for the likes of me. I can be difficult at times, as you know."

The reverend laughed. "High spirited, perhaps."

"I think we need a trial period to see if we both can adjust to this. I know that living together is frowned upon by the church, but this is a big decision and I don't want to get married and then end up divorced. And, I don't want to commit adultery."

"I see. Well, some define adultery as one married person having relations with someone other than their spouse. Others consider living together outside the sanctity of marriage as adultery." He finished his coffee and poured another cup, topping hers off, too.

Mutzi took another drink, mulling over the explanation. "What if we didn't...you know...have sex?"

"Do you think you could live with him and abstain from the temptation, until you're married?"

Mutzi felt her face warm from embarrassment. "I've been celibate this long. I think I can wait another few months."

Reverend Mitch shook his head, stifling a laugh. "This is something only you and Sam can decide. I'm sure you'll work it out."

Mutzi rose and placed her cup in the sink. "Thanks for the coffee and the advice. Maybe I'll see you at church on Sunday."

He walked her to the door. "I'd like that."

Mutzi met Sam at the Connor Community Garden at noon on Tuesday as planned. She pulled her bright blue jacket snug against her body, trying to break the gale-force wind that bit into her. "Hey, kiddo. Bet you're freezing out here waiting for me."

Sam shrugged his shoulders and grinned. "I'll warm up now that you're here. Where are we going to eat?"

"Thought we'd try out something with tomatoes." She giggled. "I'm testing those superstitions out, one at a time. How about Gustavo's Pizzeria?"

"Sounds good to me. Let's get inside. Hope they serve hot chocolate."

The two made their way into the restaurant and found a corner booth. Once the waitress took their order and brought their drinks, Mutzi took off her jacket. "I went to see Reverend Mitch." She watched a sparkle light in Sam's eyes.

"Really? I'm glad to hear that."

"I talked to him about us—possibly—living together, for a while, on a trial basis."

Sam leaned in a little closer and took her hands in his. "And?"

"Well, he said it's up to us." She bit her bottom lip, hesitant to continue. "We talked about adultery, too."

"Did he think we'd be committing adultery by living together?"

Mutzi thought about it for a moment. "He never really said either way." She sat up a little straighter and took his hand. "I think I want to try it. There's just one thing."

"That's wonderful. I've been hoping you'd say yes." He planted a kiss on her lips. "What's the one thing?"

"No sex until we're married, if we decide to marry." She searched his eyes for support.

"It won't be easy, but I will respect your wishes. No sex until—wait, are we setting a date?"

"April 1. Thought that would be an appropriate date for a couple of old fools."

"How soon will you move in?"

"Not until after the holidays. I need to break the news to Marge. I hate leaving her all alone in that big old house."

"I'm pretty sure Marge will be happy for you—for us. Maybe the change will be good for her too."

"And, if this works out, I want a small wedding in the gardens. Is that okay with you?"

"It's perfect, just like you." Sam kissed her again. "I love you, Mutzi."

Chapter Twenty-Three

*T*emperatures dropped to single digits Christmas Eve morning. Marge kicked up the thermostat and grabbed a sweater from the hall closet before joining her sisters at the kitchen island. The enticing aroma of cinnamon drifted from the oven as the buns finished baking. Mugs of steaming liquid warmed their hands as they waited.

"I've already cooked the pork loin roast for tonight. We'll have fresh green beans, baked potatoes and a salad. Does that sound all right?" Marge always liked to please her sisters, especially on special occasions.

"Sounds good to me," Mutzi agreed.

"Sour cream for the potatoes?" Rose Ellen asked.

"Of course. What would you like for dessert?"

Rose Ellen's face lit up. "I'm partial to your pineapple upside down cake."

Marge walked to the pantry to check for supplies. "I can do that." The oven timer dinged and she picked up the mitts. "I was thinking dinner at six since we'll be going to midnight services."

Mutzi refilled her coffee cup. "After I eat one of

those rolls, I'm going to the town square for a few last minute things. Need anything?"

Marge glanced around the room. "Think I've got everything covered."

Rose Ellen nibbled on her bottom lip, then announced, "I'm meeting Roberto for lunch."

Marge swirled icing on top of the steamy dish, then placed it on a trivet in the center of the table. "Again? You're seeing a lot of this curator. Is this about the ring—or something else?"

Rose Ellen helped herself to a hot roll, dripping the gooey icing on her fingertip. "Ow."

Mutzi shook her head. "Just can't wait, can you?"

Rose Ellen licked her finger and then picked up her knife and fork. "Roberto and I enjoy each other's company."

"He's still got the ring, right?" Mutzi didn't want any more bad luck to happen to her family. "Tell him to keep it."

Marge held her tongue on the subject. "It's Christmas Eve and we're going to have a wonderful day." She stood and took her dishes to the sink. "I've got some preparations to attend to for tonight. Be sure to be back here for dinner at six."

After Mutzi and Rose Ellen left the house, Marge went into the den and studied the area trying to decide how to arrange the seating for their gift opening.

A large blue spruce took up much of the room. She flicked the switch and lit the multi-colored lights, illuminating the silver and gold ornaments. The popcorn strings added a festive touch, but her favorite was the glittery white angel perched at the top, a treasure from her childhood.

There was a time when they would have sat on the floor on cushions, but age had ruled out that option. She decided to arrange three chairs, with a snack table next to each, near the fireplace. They'd have enough room to exchange gifts comfortably. Satisfied with the decision, she moved to the dining room and began setting the table.

Marge kept tissues in the pocket of her apron, knowing the tears would flow, no matter how hard she fought to keep them away. George's passing pained her as much this year as it had the first and the eight years since. He would have been the one helping her retrieve the china and spreading the linen tablecloth. She stood in front of the hutch, now upright thanks to Paul's help, and wept, glad her sisters weren't there to witness it.

Marge dried her eyes and pulled open the glass door, selecting four table settings. She'd found some lovely replacements at the antique store in the town square that nearly matched her broken ones. The extra seat at the table would remain empty, a tradition she continued each year to honor George. Her sisters had accepted the gesture without question or comment.

Dinner dishes were washed, dried and put away. Marge took off her apron and suggested they move to the den to open gifts.

Each of the sisters removed their gifts from under the tree.

Mutzi looked around the room and smiled at Marge. "You've had a busy day, Sis."

Marge flipped a switch on the stereo, turned the volume low, and played some instrumental Christmas music, adding a special touch to the evening. "Who wants to start?"

"I do!" Rose Ellen gave each sister two packages, leaving two sets of identical ones on her table. "Let's open them together." The quizzical look from them indicated an explanation was needed. "You'll understand when you see what I made."

Marge examined the silver wrapping paper with the perfect creases and blue ribbon bow. "It's too pretty to unwrap."

Rose Ellen held up the smallest package. "Let's open this one first. It's not homemade, but we'll need it for the second one."

Marge slipped a finger under the ribbon and popped it off. Her sisters followed. She did the same with the paper and opened the flap on the box revealing a blue and white bird with a hook at the bottom. "That's so pretty."

Rose Ellen stood. "Let me have them." She took all three to the mantel, moving a few of Marge's decorations to make room for the birds. "Now open the next one." She stood smiling, waiting to see their expressions.

Inside the second package was a quilted Christmas stocking with Marge's name embroidered on the cuff. It had a sapphire blue background and a wintery-white manger scene.

Marge held up the stocking and studied it, checking the seams. "Oh, Rose Ellen, it's beautiful. You did a fine job."

Mutzi chuckled as she watched Rose Ellen open her package. "See, you've got the McGilvray artistic touch in you, too."

"Maybe I do." The smile faded from Rose Ellen's face. "I've always admired the lovely things you two make. I know I don't always show it, but I cherish them." She took a deep breath and turned to Mutzi. "I have a small tree in the corner of my bedroom with every ornament you've ever given me."

Mutzi stared at her sister. "You're kidding. I always

envisioned you tossing mine into the trash when you got home."

Rose Ellen tilted her head. "I'm sorry if I gave you that impression. I treasure them." She reached across and squeezed Mutzi's hand.

"I'll be darn. That's nice. Thanks."

Rose Ellen nodded. "I didn't know you wanted to go to college. I guess I left by the time you graduated and I never gave it much thought."

Mutzi's eyes glistened as if she were holding back tears. "I shouldn't have said some of that stuff the other day. It wasn't your fault. It was mine." She drew in a deep breath. "That was a long time ago. What would I do with a degree at my age?"

"You could teach us all a few things with your computer knowledge. Is that how you knew so much about all those fancy gadgets on April's car? I'm still amazed about that."

Marge watched the tenderness between her sisters and added, "Seems we don't talk near enough. There are so many things we don't know about each other." She held up her stocking and smiled, admiring the perfect seams. "Who knew you could sew?"

"I surprised myself."

"I was also surprised to see you got a passport, Sis. I didn't know you wanted to travel. Where would you like to go?"

"Well, I've always loved the romantic notion of touring Italy and France. Without a man who feels the same, seems a waste of money." Rose Ellen heaved a sigh.

Mutzi frowned. "You've been so independent. I never thought you'd want someone to tie you down." She met Rose Ellen's eyes. "I've always admired how brave you are."

"Brave. Huh. That's just a front. I'm not brave at all. I'm lonely, or at least I have been...until I met Roberto." Rose Ellen fingered the soft fabric. "We share the same dreams about traveling."

Marge smiled. "That's wonderful. I'm looking forward to meeting him tomorrow."

"I think you'll like him. He's very charming."

Rose Ellen stood and took the stockings from her sisters, hanging them on the bird hooks, then sat down again.

A smile spread across Mutzi's face as she shook her head. "I can't believe how things are changing." She took a deep breath and turned to Marge. "You go ahead and do yours next."

Each year Mutzi merely tolerated their tradition, but tonight, she seemed different, almost cheerful about the exchange. The change in her twin's mood pleased Marge. "Okay. I will." Marge handed Rose Ellen a red and white striped box secured by a white ribbon.

Rose Ellen tore into her package. When Marge grunted, she looked up. "Oh, was I supposed to wait for Mutzi?"

Marge chuckled. "You're worse than a child. Go ahead."

Inside the box was a black beaded clutch. "Yes!" Rose Ellen held up the purse. "I need this to go with my New Year's Eve outfit. Thank you."

"I know. I tried to make it like the one you showed me."

Rose Ellen examined the impeccable stitching. "You made this?"

Marge nodded. "Look inside."

Unzipping the purse, Rose Ellen let out a gasp. "Where on earth did you find it?"

A broad grin spread across Marge's face. "I didn't. It was Thelma. She was getting ready for the after-Christmas sale and pulled all the holiday items out of a bin. Your wallet was at the bottom."

Rose Ellen checked inside it. "It's all here. Even my money."

Mutzi chuckled. "Of course it is. There aren't too many thieves in this town."

"I never thought I'd see it again. Thank you."

"You're welcome. Be sure to stop by and tell Thelma thanks, too."

Marge glanced at Mutzi. "This one's for you." She handed her sister a large box with a festive yellow bow made from curly ribbon tied around snowman wrapping paper.

Mutzi lifted the lid. Inside was a colorful patchwork quilt. "Hey. I recognize this material." Her eyes lit up as she touched each square.

"I hope you don't mind. I found a box of your clothes in the attic."

Mutzi pointed to a bright orange block. "This was a sweatshirt from my senior year." Her fingers moved to the next one. "And this was one of Sam's shirts he gave to me."

Marge watched as Mutzi relived each piece of history. "Are you upset that I cut up your clothes?"

Mutzi eyes widened. "Are you kidding, Sis? You immortalized my memories." She stood and crossed the room, surprising Marge with a bear hug. "It's beautiful. I love it."

She went back to her chair and held the quilt for a few minutes, admiring her sister's handiwork.

Impatient as always, Rose Ellen interrupted the intimate moment. "What about your gifts for us?"

Mutzi set down the quilt and picked up a large gift bag embossed with flocked candy canes, handing it to Marge. "Open yours first."

Marge removed the tissue paper. Mutzi stepped

closer and helped pull the padded photo album out of the tight fitting bag. Marge's mouth dropped open when she looked at the cover. The front of the album held a picture, imprinted on fabric, of Marge and George standing in front of their house. "How in the world did you do this?" She stared at Mutzi in disbelief.

"That computer, the one you refuse to use. It can do amazing things."

Rose Ellen got up and moved in close enough to see the dozens of photos inside. "I don't think I've ever seen these pictures. When were they taken?"

Mutzi grinned. "A few years ago I got into the digital camera craze. With the advances today, all you have to do is select which ones you want to print, send off an electronic order, they print them out and mail them to you. They also print them on fabric. Pretty cool, huh?"

"I'm speechless. This is such a thoughtful gift." Marge hugged Mutzi. "Maybe you'll have to teach me how to use that computer thing."

"Just say when." Mutzi picked up the second bag and handed it to Rose Ellen. "This is for you."

Rose Ellen remained standing as she unwrapped the framed document. A picture of the ring she'd once seen in the display case at the Gold Museum was centered at the top. She glanced from the gift to Mutzi.

"What in the world?"

"Read it out loud."

The History of the Gold Miner Ring

December 18, 2017

The first Gold Rush Days Festival was held in 1954. Its purpose was to bring attention to the century-long history of gold mining in Dahlonega. A variety of activities—including spinning, churning and making moonshine—brought folks from across the miles. Inspired by the fashions of the 1830's—the year of the first United States gold rush, which occurred in Dahlonega, Georgia—men grew impressive beards and women wore long dresses and old fashioned bonnets for the celebration.

One of the most beloved events during the festival was the crowning of the King and Queen of Gold Rush. In honor the event, a local jeweler fashioned a pair of cuff links depicting a man panning for gold and presented them to the king.

A similar ring was also bequeathed to the queen. She wore it with pride until 1967, when the Dahlonega Gold Museum opened. At that time, she offered to loan the ring to the museum for display.

Recently, some community members have voiced concerns about the disposition of the historical items. My research revealed the cuff links were melted down and sold when the king experienced financial difficulties.

Descendants of the queen, who wish to remain anonymous, have verified that the original gold miner ring was returned to the family upon the queen's death, and it remains in their possession as of the date of this document.

In the fall of 1969, Mr. Bernard McGilvray, a volunteer at the gold museum, commissioned the jeweler to create a replica of the ring as a gift for his daughter, Rose Ellen McGilvray. Unfortunately, before she received it, Mr. McGilvray died after suffering a brief illness. Through a series of unfortunate events, the ring did not come into her possession until recently.

This document serves as official clarification of the gold miner ring's origin and disposition.

Signed,
Victoria Bridges, Historian

Rose Ellen stared at her Mutzi, her mouth agape. "How in the world did you get this?"

Marge moved closer. "May I see it?" She smiled as she looked at the letter printed on fine linen paper, preserved in a stunning silver frame. "Mutzi told you that Victoria would know, but you didn't listen to her."

"You did?" Rose stepped next to Mutzi and touched her arm. "I'm sorry. You—are remarkable. You never cease to amaze me, in a good way. Thank you."

"Glad you like it. I couldn't have you thinking Daddy stole it for you. You're not *that* special." Mutzi nudged Rose Ellen and let out a giggle.

Rose Ellen laughed. "Well, I must have been pretty special for him to have it commissioned for me."

Mutzi shook her head. "By the way, I gave a copy of the letter to Thelma. Should take care of the nasty gossip."

Marge set the framed document down and picked up her glass. "What a remarkable evening. I'd like to offer a toast. May faith, courage and love keep us strong and may all our dreams come true."

Chapter Twenty-Four

A light dusting of snow covered the ground overnight. Marge paused by the picture window and cherished a quiet moment. A white Christmas made it feel extra special and brought thoughts of George to mind. Each time it snowed, he'd delighted in clearing the sidewalk, catching snow on his tongue and laughing heartily. She was pleased she didn't have to worry about having the sidewalk shoveled today.

Marge had delegated the task of setting the table "Christmas pretty" to her sisters. It wasn't long before she heard Mutzi and Rose Ellen squabbling in the dining room. Marge peeked around the corner and watched in silence as the sister's fussed at each other.

"Use Mother's white tablecloth with the silver bells cross-stitched on the edges."

Mutzi wasted no time spreading her choice across the extended table. "The red one's more colorful. Get the green napkins."

Rose Ellen wrinkled her nose. "I think the white ones look better."

Tired of the bickering, Marge walked into the room and settled the argument. "That looks fine." She pulled open the china hutch door and motioned to Rose Ellen to help. "We'll need eight place settings, and two glasses for each guest, one for wine and one for tea or water."

A clatter at the front door drew their attention. A large floral arrangement and a mound of gifts nearly obscured the guests' faces. Marge scurried toward the foyer and opened the door for April and Paul. She took the fragrant, oblong arrangement of red and white mums and placed it in the middle of the table, then checked to see if the arrangement needed water. "It's beautiful. Thank you both."

Once they removed their coats, Marge offered them a hug. "I'm delighted to see the two of you back together. Merry Christmas."

"Looks like you've got everyone working." April kissed her aunt's cheek and greeted her mother and Mutzi. "What can I do to help?"

Marge glanced around trying to decide what else needed to be done. "How about getting the box of silverware and finish setting the table?"

April raised a hand. "I'm on it."

The lovely centerpiece finalized Marge's indecision about whether to serve buffet or family style. "Rose Ellen, I changed my mind. Would you take all the plates to the kitchen island?"

Her sister opened her mouth as if she was going to complain, but pressed her lips together instead, and picked up the china.

Paul followed Marge into the kitchen, rubbing his hands together. "What can I do?"

Marge pointed to the counter. "How about arranging the turkey and spiral-sliced honey ham on that platter?"

"I think I can handle that."

Marge made a mental list of everything she needed to set out on the substantial island. Each person would find their favorites. Rose Ellen loved Waldorf salad, a must for all special occasions. April drooled over Marge's mustard potato salad. Paul devoured her broccoli and cheese casserole whenever he came around.

The enticing smell of fried bacon lingered in the room, Marge's special touch added to the green bean dish Sam requested. Desserts lined the counter next to the stove, including Mutzi's much loved Rice Krispy treats with Santa faces etched in white icing.

Sam and Roberto arrived at the same time. Roberto carried a triple layer chocolate cake and sat it next to the pumpkin and apple pies, her favorites.

Satisfied with her spread, Marge invited all of the

guests to find a place at the celebratory table and remain standing while she led the group in prayer.

"I think it's appropriate if each of us gives thanks for the blessings in our lives." She looked toward the den where George's picture hung. "For family and friends with us today and to those forever engraved in my heart, I pray the blessings of peace and love forever protect you." She turned to Rose Ellen and nodded for her to follow.

Rose Ellen cleared her throat and looked around the table. "I'm thankful for all of my family and friends, too. I'm not sure if this is the right time to say this, but I can't wait any longer. I've sold my business."

Marge's eyes widened and she stole a glance at Mutzi, whose mouth hung open. "You're moving back?"

"Don't worry, I'm not moving in." She turned to Roberto. "I'm not sure where we'll land, but Roberto and I are going to travel the world."

"Good for you, Mom."

Roberto went next. "Meeting questa **belissima signora** was the greatest gift I've ever received." He glanced around the room. "Now I'm blessed to meet her wonderful family. Thank you, Marge, for inviting me."

April took Paul's hand as she prepared to speak.

"All of you are so important to me, but I'm most thankful for this man." April turned and stared into Paul's eyes. "My husband."

It took a nanosecond for the words to filter through. Rose Ellen's face turned bright red. "You got...married?"

Paul kissed his wife's cheek. "Yes. We decided to elope. All the fussing about wedding arrangements distracted from what was important. We love each other and want to spend the rest of our lives together." He wrapped his arm around her shoulder. "I'm sorry if that offends anyone, but it was the right thing to do."

Congratulations briefly interrupted the prayerful messages, but soon the noise quieted down. Marge nodded to Sam. "Let's continue."

He took in a deep breath. "All my life, my heart pulled me back to Dahlonega." He focused on Mutzi as he spoke. "I'm thankful that I finally listened to it. Most of all, I'm thankful the love of my life could forgive me for leaving her." His voice cracked and he stopped speaking as he stared at Mutzi.

She glanced at him for a second and looked away. "All this touchy feely stuff makes me nervous. I'm grateful for all the food Marge cooked. Let's eat."

Everyone laughed and headed to the kitchen. While they were around the island filling their plates,

Marge poured the traditional cabernet into their glasses. As she removed her apron, ready to join her guests, she let out a deep sigh. *How fast life changes.*

Chapter Twenty-Five

*M*utzi squirmed in the front seat of Sam's car on the drive to his place, anxious to see if Clyde delivered her present for Sam. As they rounded the last bend and turned into the long driveway, her eyes focused on the small bridge that carried them over the creek bed. The solar light illuminated the bold, black letters. *Welcome to Parks' Place, Where Dreams Come True.* Sam turned to Mutzi with one brow drawn.

Mutzi bit on her bottom lip, wringing her hands waiting for his reaction.

Sam stopped the car and put it in park, exiting the vehicle with a quick pace.

Mutzi followed him, taking his arm as they stood in front of the illuminated sign. "It's your Christmas present. Do you like it?"

Sam nodded, bending down to examine the finely crafted wooden marker. "You did this for me?" He stood and drew Mutzi in close.

"Clyde Smith made it for you. He suggested adding the light."

"I love it. The words are perfect." Sam squeezed her waist and gave a peck on her cheek. "I hope I can make all *your* dreams come true."

She nestled her head on his chest and drew in the cinnamon and mint scent of his aftershave. "It wasn't easy coming up with an idea. I wanted something useful that you'd keep for years. Didn't think you needed one of my homemade crafts."

"It's perfect." He lifted her chin and planted a kiss on her lips. "Thank you."

Mutzi shivered and took Sam's hand in hers. "It's getting cold out here. Let's get inside and warm up. Maybe you can make us some hot cocoa."

Once in the house, Sam hung their coats in the hall closet and flipped a switch to light the tree. The Douglas fir, centered in front of the picture window, glowed with yellow, blue and green bubble lights. Gold ornaments hung on each limb and shiny red garland streamed up and down the entire tree. A sparkling white angel perched on the top, playing "Silent Night."

Mutzi admired the attention to detail. "For someone who just moved in, you sure did a lot of work."

Sam shook his head. "You have no idea. Wait until you see your presents." He took her hand and led her down the hall, stopping at the first door and opening it.

With the flick of a switch, the room lit revealing periwinkle walls. The ceiling resembled the night sky with stars twinkling across it. Bright yellow and pink pillows topped the green paisley bedspread. A rocking chair sat near the window, next to a corner table that held a lava lamp. The colorful wax mixture inside the glass vessel moved in fluid motion, constantly changing shapes. Mutzi broke her stare from the object that reminded her of the emotional ride she'd been on the past few weeks and met Sam's smile. "This was yours. I remember watching it for hours."

Sam nodded. "I thought it would bring you comfort."

Mutzi moved to the bed and picked up one of the pillows, caressing it like a kitten. "I'm blown away. The colors, the textures. You put so much thought into it. What a wonderful Christmas present. Thank you."

"Oh, we're not done." He took the pillow from her and set it on the bed. "Come with me." They walked down the hall to another room.

When Sam opened the door, Mutzi took a step back and covered her mouth. Her eyes widened as she looked from one corner to the other. "This is the "babe cave" I saw on the computer." She stared at Sam, her mind reeling with everything she saw. "Marge had a cow when I suggested redoing one of her rooms like this." She ambled to the multi-colored cubes and browsed the books, before shooting a puzzled look at

Sam. "These are mine."

"I hope it's all right. I asked Marge for a box of your favorites."

"It's...so thoughtful." Mutzi inched her way around the room, first touching the hammock, then working her way to the desk. "I've been so nervous about moving in. I don't conform to other people's expectations. That's just who I am." She took hold of Sam's hands. "But, you get that. You get...me. I can't believe you did all this for me."

Sam leaned in and kissed her. "I don't want you to change. I love you just as you are, a very special woman."

Mutzi closed her eyes for a moment, a sense of peace and contentment releasing the nerves she'd clenched tight until now. She believed him, completely. All her fears subsided and she squeezed his hands. "I think it's going to be okay."

"I'll do anything to make sure it is. I want us to spend the rest of our lives together."

She drew in a deep breath. "I love you, Sam Parks. I probably won't say it too often, but know that I love you." The kiss that followed sent a shiver up her spine, stimulating feelings Mutzi hadn't had since high school when her raging hormones made her want him in every way. "Think we better go get that cocoa now." She took his hand and led him out of the room.

Sam wiped his suddenly damp forehead. "Maybe some ice tea instead. It's getting pretty warm in here."

Chapter Twenty-Six

The new calendar on the wall and the absence of any Christmas decorations signaled the New Year. Mutzi sipped her tea at the kitchen island, watching Marge knead dough for an upcoming bake sale. "Life sure changes fast."

"That it does." Marge dusted a little more flour on the marbled cutting board, flipped the pastry over, and punched it with both hands. "What are you pondering? You have that look about you."

The mug twisted and turned in Mutzi's hand. "Oh, you know. A few weeks ago, this place buzzed with people. Now April's gone." She sighed. "And Rose Ellen's left on her cruise to Europe with Roberto."

Marge nodded without looking up. "She kept the lease on her Long Island apartment, and Roberto did the same with his place. They figured it would give them the freedom to return to their single life should things not work out." Marge rolled the bread into a ball and covered it with plastic wrap. "But, I don't think they will need them. They were meant for each other. You can see it in their eyes when they look at each other." Marge smiled and nodded. "Sometimes, things work out right."

Mutzi set her tea down and ran both hands through her greying hair. She rolled her shoulders, scrunching them up and relaxing them, releasing a deep sigh.

Marge turned and locked eyes with Mutzi. "What is it?"

Mutzi stood and walked to the stove to refill her cup. "Sam's ready for me to move in with him."

After a short pause, Marge asked, "Is that what you want?"

"I think so." Mutzi ran her finger around the rim of the cup. "Sam knows how I feel about living together before we're married." She took another sip.

"I know you love him, but do you want to marry him?"

She nibbled on her lower lip. "I do. Always have."

"Is he ready to get married again?"

Mutzi stood and turned away, pacing the room. "He's asked me three times."

Marge reached to touch her sister's arm as she passed her. "Then what's the problem?"

"Look at me. I'm not easy to live with. I know that."

Her sister smiled. "You'll both adjust. You will. Two people in love find a way."

Mutzi nodded her head, wanting to believe, but still having reservations.

"Do you think George and I were a perfect fit from

the start? I drove him crazy with my need for everything to be in its place and done according to my whims." She paused. "He'd come in from work and leave his shoes in the foyer, and I'd yell at him." Marge chuckled. "After a little while, we adjusted to each other. He stopped leaving his shoes where they didn't belong and I tried not to shout if he forgot."

"You know what Sam gave me for my Christmas present?"

"What?"

"He fixed up two of the rooms in his house, just for me." She stopped moving, wanting to find words to describe how much thought he'd put into everything. "One is a bedroom for me to stay in. You should see how he decorated it." She couldn't help but smile as she spoke. "The other one is a babe cave. It's painted in bright colors and it even has an indoor hammock facing the window. Did he show it to you when you gave him the books?"

"No. He wanted you to be the first to see it. He must love you a lot to go to all that effort."

"I know he does. He's a really good guy."

"So why not give it a trial run? A month or two?"

"What would the ladies in the Woman's Club think? Two unmarried people living together?"

"A lot of older couples do that now, for financial reasons. Besides, I've never known you to give a darn about what they thought. Why start now?" She tipped her head, locking eyes with Mutzi. "What else is bothering you?"

Mutzi met Marge's stare. "Leaving you all alone in this big old house."

Marge rose and wrapped her sister in her arms. "I'll be okay. God's not done with me yet. Maybe he'll send some poor soul that needs a bed and a good meal my way."

"That's what I'm afraid of. You've got too big a heart."

"I'll be fine, Mutzi. I want you to be happy and start living your life. You put it on hold for too many years."

Mutzi studied Marge's face. "You're sure?"

"I'm positive."

"Maybe I'll give Sam a call."

When Mutzi left, Marge wandered into the study. "Well, George. It looks like it's going to be just the two of us. Such a waste of our lovely Victorian. I liked it much better when Mutzi and April lived with us. April brought friends over almost every day." She picked up a dust cloth and polished the woodwork. "We always had company coming or going. I don't think I can manage it by myself. What will I do if there's no one to cook for?"

Marge wiped the already dust free mantle, then went to the console in the corner of the room. With the greatest of care, she lifted the arm of the antiquated stereo and placed the needle on the record. The Tennessee Waltz soothed her spirits and she closed her eyes, dreaming of her and George swaying to the beat. When the song finished, she lifted the arm and shut off the music.

The weight of her mood became too heavy to carry. Marge eased in the leather chair and folded her hands on her lap. "I've been thinking, George. Remember when April stayed with us while she attended college? It was so delightful to have all that bouncy, blissful energy to fill the rooms. She was happy here, wasn't she, George?"

Marge fiddled with the cloth. "I bet there are other girls, you know, on the campus who are lonely living in a dorm. Even if they have a roommate, they probably miss their mothers. Oh, and of course their fathers, too. But most girls miss their mother."

Marge sat, as if waiting for an answer. "I'm thinking about opening our home up to a few of them. I wish you were here to tell me what you think." She took a piece of paper from the desk and started doodling. "It's so hard to know what to do. I just know I can't stay in this house by myself." As if George were answering her, she continued, "Oh, don't worry, I'd never consider selling it. You worked too hard to buy it for me. If only you could give me a sign."

Chapter Twenty-Seven

*M*arge finished her morning coffee and wiped down the kitchen island. She glanced at the clock and groaned. With every household chore completed, and dinner already in the crockpot, the day would drag. She was grateful when the phone rang. "Hello?"

"Mrs. Margaret McGilvray Ledbetter?" The familiar voice quivered as the woman spoke.

Marge smiled to herself. Only one woman in town insisted on calling her by her maiden *and* married name—the Director of Residence Life at the University of Northern Georgia. "Yes, Mrs. Brown. What can I do for you?"

"Would you have room in your schedule to meet with me this morning? I have a proposal to discuss."

"Of course. I'm free all day. What time would be good for you?" Marge didn't feel the need to ask what the meeting entailed. Whatever service the college needed, whether it came from the Woman's Club or her personal time, she willingly provided it.

"Let's meet at the faculty lounge at ten."

"That's perfect. I'll see you then." Marge hung up and walked into the study to George's picture and kissed it. "I bet you told her to call. You still know how to lift my spirits. I don't know how you do it from so far away." Marge thought for a minute. "Perhaps, you're not so far at all." She grabbed her purse and headed out the door.

The sun broke through the gray skies and warmed Marge's back as she walked across the college parking lot. She loved being on campus. There was an energy, an electricity, emanating from the youthful surroundings. *Maybe I should sign up for one of the senior citizen computer programs.* The thought of returning to school excited and frightened her at the same time, but she needed something to fill the empty days ahead.

Marge entered the lounge and greeted the woman who'd summoned her. Mrs. Eleanor Brown—her white hair pulled into a tight bun and her sky-blue blouse buttoned to the very top—stood and extended her hand.

"Please, sit. Thank you for coming in today. I'll make this as brief as possible. I know you keep a busy schedule."

"Actually, things have slowed down a bit with the holidays ending. How can I help you, today?"

The director settled in her chair and opened a manila folder, withdrawing a picture of three young women. "These lovely ladies are triplets."

Marge loved the way Mrs. Brown handled business. No aimless chatter. Got right to the point, although there were times when Marge would have enjoyed getting to know the woman better. She glanced from the photo to the director. "Triplets?" The three teens were as different as she and Mutzi. "How interesting."

"They hope to attend our college, if we can provide accommodations for them. They wish to room together."

Marge nodded in anticipation of the request. *There are some things one just knows.* "And your dorms are at full capacity." She didn't wait for Mrs. Brown to finish. "I would love to have them stay with me."

The director pushed back her chair and stood, her eyes bulging from their sockets. "How did you know what I was going to ask?"

Marge rose, considering whether or not to reveal her earlier talk with George, but decided against it. "You could call it a woman's intuition."

"We'll need to discuss the arrangements. I've made a list of items we'll need to speak about and there will be additional compensation by the college for your troubles."

"Don't be silly. I wouldn't think of taking anything from the college. Students rent rooms off campus all the time, don't they?"

"Yes, they do."

"Then why would this be any different? Am I missing something?"

Mrs. Brown fiddled with the bun on her head, her eyes darted up and down the list she'd made. "I'm afraid I wasn't prepared for this to go so smoothly. I've never asked someone to open their home to students before, and I would never consider doing it myself. Are you sure?"

"Absolutely. When will they arrive?"

"The girls and their parents live in Atlanta, but they are staying at the Dahlonega Square Hotel."

"Please give them my address and phone number. They may stop by any time this afternoon. I'd love to meet the parents and reassure them they've made the right decision."

Mrs. Brown extended her hand and shook her head in disbelief. "Thank you, Margaret."

She called me by my first name. I really did unnerve her. Marge smiled all the way back to her car. A little part of her enjoyed startling the director. Her mind raced ahead, thinking of all the special touches she could add to the rooms to make the girls feel welcomed.

The doorbell rang promptly at two. The delectable scent of cinnamon filled the kitchen. One of Marge's favorite coffee cakes cooled on the kitchen island. Heading to the door, Marge passed the study and blew George a kiss, thanking him again for his intervention and reminding herself how blessed her life could continue to be, even without his physical presence.

Chapter Twenty-Eight

*T*ulips and daffodil lined the sidewalk of the quaint park on Main Street. The fountain spilled its water like a babbling brook. Sam adjusted his red paisley tie and straightened the grey pin-striped suit he'd bought for the occasion.

Sam and Mutzi planned a quiet wedding with only her immediate family. Although no wedding invitations had been mailed out, the surrounding streets were lined with dozens of well-wishers. The crowd continued to grow as he waited for Mutzi and Marge to arrive. They'd come to see his soon-to-be bride and he couldn't wait for her to see their celebratory efforts. For someone who felt challenged all her life to gain friends in her town, Mutzi would soon realize how many people she'd truly touched over the years.

The affirmation of the town's affection for Mutzi's uniqueness was evident. Like a float in a parade, every inch of the white gazebo had been covered in multicolored roses. Their sweet fragrance filled the air as the sun shone overhead. An arch of carnations would

greet her when she arrived, as would the colorful balloons each on-looker carried.

For the second time in years, Mutzi had agreed to let
her sister select her clothes, a creamy white, tailored
pantsuit with a turquoise shell. Recognizing her need
for bright color, Marge bedazzled white tennis shoes
with a rainbow of colored beads and added a yellow
sash as a belt around her waist.

A band of daisies was woven into Mutzi's pinned
up silver hair. She'd even allowed Marge to apply a
touch of blush to her cheeks and the faintest shade of
rose to her lips. Mutzi appreciated Marge's efforts in
making her feel special. "Maybe I should let you dress
me more often."

"You look beautiful." Marge re-tied the ribbon
around Mutzi's waist. "I'm so happy for you. You've always deserved this, and so much more."

Mutzi's eyes grew moist. "Let's get this show on the
road."

When they walked outside to get in Marge's car, a
white limousine awaited them. "Oh, for heaven's
sakes. Sam shouldn't have wasted his money for a few
blocks."

Marge grinned and ushered Mutzi into the car. "Of
course he should. You're worth it. He's a lucky man to

have you as his wife."

"Such silliness. Should have gone to the Justice of the Peace and been done with it."

The familiar driver, a man who lived around the corner, closed the door and got behind the wheel. He glanced in the rearview mirror before taking off. "Looking mighty pretty, Ms. Mutzi."

Mutzi's cheeks burned with the compliment. "Just drive, Tom." When he didn't take a direct route to the park, she barked at him, "Where the heck you going? You getting paid by the mile?"

"Have to avoid the traffic jam." Tom chuckled as they rounded another corner and the massive crowd came into view.

Mutzi's face hardened, her brows furrowed as she shot a look from the line of people to her sister. "What the he—heck is going on?"

Marge looked at her and took her hand. "I know you wanted a small wedding, but once you and Sam applied for the license, word got out. Everyone wanted to celebrate with you. Please don't be upset."

Mutzi mulled over all the fussing they'd done for her and Sam. Her face softened into a half smile. "I'll be darn. Who knew they cared?"

When the car stopped, Tom hurried to open the door, but Mutzi beat him to it. He extended an arm for her to take and she obliged.

April and Paul grinned sheepishly as they stepped aside and revealed two unexpected visitors. Rose Ellen hurried forward with Roberto close behind. "This is so exciting. I love surprises. Are you surprised?"

Mutzi nodded. "I thought you two were cruising the Mediterranean?"

"We wouldn't have missed this for the world." Rose wrapped an arm around her sister and squeezed.

Mutzi noticed the ring on Rose Ellen's right hand, but didn't flinch. It no longer held power over her, if it ever really did. Being with Sam made her feel safe and complete. They'd adjusted to each other much easier than either had anticipated. The more confident she'd grown in their relationship, the more her superstitions had disappeared. The need to maintain the daily rituals that restricted what she ate and where she stepped had disappeared, along with the concerns about the gold miner ring.

Reverend Mitch raised a hand to quiet the crowd. When they hushed, Mutzi processioned through the floral arbor toward Sam as he sang, "You are my sunshine, my only sunshine..." His baritone voice resonated across the town square.

Tears welled in Mutzi's eyes. Never in her wildest dreams did she think this day would happen. She glanced up to the sky and gave a nod for her blessing, thankful the long journey had brought them back together, at last.

When the song ended, Sam handed the microphone to the preacher and turned toward Mutzi. Reverend Mitch lifted his hands toward the sky and spoke. "Two souls, destined to be united as one, stand before us today. The master plan is seldom revealed to us. Often, it is not what we desire, nor what we think we need, nor does it happen when we think it should, but for those who endure the journey with faith and hope, the rewards are boundless. Let us begin."

The two exchanged their vows and when the reverend gave the word, Sam drew Mutzi close and kissed her. "My love, my forever love." He kissed her again with the passion of a man who'd waited a lifetime for his true love.

For the next half hour, Sam and Mutzi greeted what seemed like every citizen in Dahlonega. She couldn't believe they were all here, for her. And, for once, she didn't have to fake a smile. In fact, it remained daubed on her face long after the crowd dispersed.

The unpretentious ceremony was everything Mutzi had hoped for and more. The fact that Rose Ellen and Roberto interrupted their trip and the unexpected crowd of friends and neighbors who decorated and brought balloons to celebrate with them, filled her heart with joy. None of this would have been possible had Sam not been encouraged by his late wife to return to Dahlonega. She'd be forever grateful to the woman she'd never met.

April placed a hand on the bride's shoulder. "Can I get a picture of you with Mom and Aunt Marge?"

Mutzi nodded. "I'd like that." She stepped in between her sisters and smiled. "Life sure can change fast."

The End

If you enjoyed Mutzi, Marge, and Rose Ellen's story, stay tuned for book two.

Even fertile ground can unearth skeletons.

Researching ancestry creates friction and unexpected twists for the McGilvray sisters in their next novel, *The Dahlonega Sisters, Veins of Gold.*

Coming soon!

Delightful venues in and around Dahlonega as mentioned in this book

Fresh n Low grocery store https://www.freshnlow.com

The Fudge Factory candy store
http://dahlonegafudgefactory.com/

Dahlonega General store https://dahlonegageneralstore.com/

Giggle Monkey Toys https://www.gigglemonkeytoys.com/

Woody's Barber Sh91 N Park 2062 Public Square

St. Luke's Church 91 N Park St

Gustavo's Pizza 16 Public Square S

Dahlonega Gold Museum http://dahlonega.org/historic-downtown-4/dahlonega-gold-museum

Dahlonega Visitor Center 135 Park

PJ Rusted Buffalo Leather Store 98 Public Square N

Dahlonega Community House 111 N Park St

Shenanigan's Irish Pub http://www.theshenaniganspub.com/

Georgia Wine and Oyster Bar 19 Chestatee St

The Smith House https://smithhouse.com/

Montaluce Estates & Winery http://montaluce.com/

University of North Georgia https://ung.edu/

Connor Community Garden Corner of N Chestatee and Warwick Sts

Other venues mentioned outside of Dahlonega

Scotts Downtown, Gainesville, GA

https://www.scottsdowntown.com/

Sun Dial (Westin Hotel), Atlanta, GA
https://www.sundialrestaurant.com/

Gibbs Gardens, Ballground, GA 30107
https://www.gibbsgardens.com/

Note: Magical Threads and Ole ' Mountain Collectables and Wine Store have since closed

There are dozens—no—probably hundreds of other interesting places in Dahlonega that deserve to be mentioned, however my characters chose to share these while they told me their story. (It's hard to imagine, but it's true. Other writers will understand.)

Acknowledgements

Eternal optimist, that's me. Always searching for a silver lining when dark clouds gloom overhead, rummaging through the unpleasant to find the positive. What's often obscured by dread, distress, and disappointment makes me search for an amiable, welcoming, and hopefully, a satisfying outcome.

That's exactly how The Dahlonega Sisters came to life. A dear friend shared a troublesome experience and suggested it would make a great book. Unprepared to write the tender and very personal story, I offered my 'silver lining' version that incorporated some details from her recollections and provided a blissful ending. Fortunately, Vincenne Caruso, approved, and I'm so happy she did. I raise my rose-colored glass in appreciation to you, Mutzi, for trusting me with your pain, sorrow and fears. I hope the pleasant ending brings you peace and joy.

A huge thanks to my brother and sister-in-law, Bob and Lana Hootselle, who have spent endless hours gathering information, proofing my many drafts, and even driving around Dahlonega's town square taking pictures and checking details. You've never doubted my efforts and have always been two of my biggest supporters. For that and so much more, I'm very grateful.

To my Round Table Writers critique friends,

Tammy Lough, Denise Judd, Nicki Jacobsmeyer, Donna Mork Reed, and Jeanne Felfe, know that each of you influenced my manuscript in a unique way, making it shine with your wonderful suggestions. Thank you for the time and effort you put into every critique you provide.

To my dearest friends, Rose Ellen Koutsobinas and Denise Judd, your constant support and interest have helped me to find that silver lining whenever the clouds gathered. Bless you both for listening, caring and providing hugs and wine whenever the going got tough.

Proofreading takes many eyes and keen attention to detail. Thanks to Rose Ellen Koutsobinas, Mary Beida, Denise Judd and my daughter, Laura How, for devoting so many hours to reading each word, checking for every missed period, and finding all my missing quotation marks.

To Jeanne Felfe, I owe more than words can express. Without your hand-holding me through the complicated process of editing, formatting, publishing, and marketing, this book would never have made it this far. Your patience, detailed guidelines, gracious availability when I called, text or emailed, and constant reassurance that I could do this meant the difference between failure and fulfilling a dream.

To my daughter, Laura J. How, thank you for listening to my endless ramblings and for proofing my final product. You are the best daughter a mother could ever have and I love you.

Finally, to my loving husband and partner of forty-seven years, Lavern Lee (Wart) How, thank you for the many hours you spent alone while I labored away in front of my laptop, and for the hundreds of texts and emails that interrupted our days and nights. Wish I could tell you it won't happen again, but we both know it will. Love you forever and a day.

A Note to Readers,

I am honored you chose to read *The Dahlonega Sisters, The Gold Miner Ring*. I hope you'll visit again when *The Dahlonega Sisters, Veins of Gold*, makes its way to publication.

Part of the joy of writing is connecting with readers. I'd love to hear your feedback. I'm always looking for ways to bring satisfaction and joy to the reader and I can't think of a better way to make that happen than to hear it from you at:

https://authordianemhow.com
https://www.bookbub.com/profile/diane-m-how
https://www.amazon.com/author/dianemhow
https://www.facebook.com/diane.how.9

Reviews and recommendations make a huge difference, especially for a first time novelist like me. Sharing what you like with family and friends is the best way of spreading the word. I hope you'll find time to let others know about *The Dahlonega Sisters*, by leaving a review on Amazon, Goodreads, Barnes and Noble, Bookbub, or other social media outlet. Just a sentence or two would be appreciated. Thank you for your support.

With my deepest appreciation,

Diane

ABOUT THE AUTHOR

Diane M How lives in St. Peters, Missouri with her husband of forty-seven years. Being retired affords her the time to indulge in her passion for writing on a daily basis. Many of her award winning short stories and poems can be found in anthologies published by Saturday Writer, a well-known and supportive writers guild that maintains more than a hundred members. This is Diane's first published novel, but hopefully not her last.

Made in the USA
Monee, IL
28 October 2021